TALES FROM FADREAMA

Candace N. Coonan

Book 5
Twilight Revolution

Order this book online at www.trafford.com
or email orders@trafford.com

Most Trafford titles are also available at major online book retailers.

Printed in the United States of America.

ISBN: 978-1-4669-3257-9 (sc)
ISBN: 978-1-4669-3256-2 (hc)
ISBN: 978-1-4669-3258-6 (e)

Library of Congress Control Number: 2012907198

Trafford rev. 04/26/2012

 www.trafford.com

North America & international
toll-free: 1 888 232 4444 (USA & Canada)
phone: 250 383 6864 ✦ fax: 812 355 4082

CONTENTS

Dedication

For Japan

Preface

*I*T HAS BEEN QUITE a few years since Book 4 was released and at long last, the final part of the journey is complete. You hold within your hands, Book 5, the last tale from Fadreama. While there is some sadness in ending this journey, there is also anticipation and excitement at what new things are to come. And if you really think about it, there are no endings, only transformations.

Dawn and her friends face the biggest challenge of their young lives and I like to think that they face it with grace, trust and faith. They do not know how everything will end, or what will happen after that, but they continue onward with the knowledge that there is something greater than themselves at work. Just as there is darkness in everyones' hearts, there is also light and it is this very characteristic that makes people human.

My husband, Shuji, did the cover sketch for this book, which (if you hadn't figured it out yet) is supposed to be the work of the character Ian. The cover sketches are pages from his sketch book. I am so honoured to have collaborated with my true love and I love him more every single day. I also want to thank my son, Kai, for bringing me the greatest joy of my life—motherhood! The interior map of Fadreama is the original map done by the talented Rhonda Trider. Thank you!

I want to put a little note here about editing. Yes, I know there are typos and such in this book and others. I know, I know, I know. Please have the heart to overlook them and just enjoy the story. Or, if you enjoy documenting typos, do so, whatever makes you happy—I just don't want phone calls about it, thank you.

I truly hope you will enjoy the conclusion of this series that has certainly changed my life. I look forward to all the new stories that are to come throughout my journey in this lifetime. If there is one thing I would have you take away from this series and hold in your heart (long after the *Tales* have been forgotten), it is that if you strip away everything from the world, all the divisions, all the frills, all the wants, needs, countries, power, races, religions, money . . . everything, you are left with only one element—love. Love is all there is. Period. Eliminate all the excesses and reduce the entire universe down to its core and you will find love. That's all there is.

Candace Coonan Osawa
April 5, 2012

The Sacred Balance

Illuminate like the FIRE,
But don't burn like the blaze.
For who can see anything,
Through the smoke and the haze?

Flow like the WATER,
But don't crash like the wave.
For with too much force,
No one can be saved.

Fly high like the AIR,
But don't destroy like the gale.
For the seduction of power,
Will cause you to fail.

Root deep in the EARTH,
But don't spread like the weed.
For in grasping too much,
You shall be consumed only by greed.

Out of the dark,
Light is breaking free,
Revealing all that is destined to be.

The Shadows swarm towards the hive of light,
Not understanding its loving might.
It draws them inside,
Only to show…
Ethereal forgiveness and love's cleansing glow.

In the void and the dark,
A tiny light flickers bright,
An intention of love,
The Power's might.

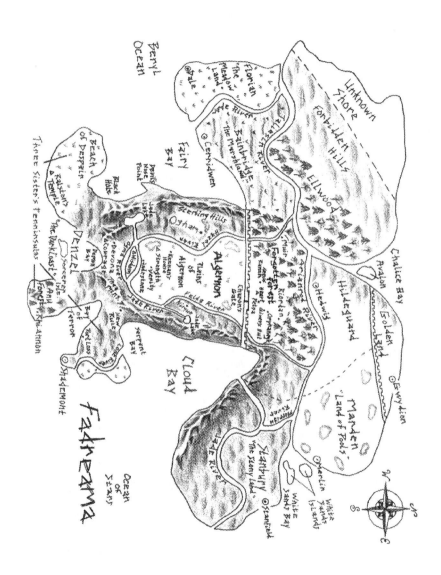

Prologue

Syoho's Voice

OUR WORLD WILL SOON be no more. At least, it will not be as we know it now. I fear the days of Fadreama have passed. Already the change—the transformation—has begun. It is like a mighty storm that cannot be stopped. The most we can do is live in the time that is left . . .

From this change, there will be no return. It is . . . the will of the Power beyond the stars—not mine. *My* will has become very human and very much like Alice's. However, the fact remains that I am Syoho and as such, sworn to serve the Power. Though I do not understand the 'why,' I will abide. After all, everything changes in its proper course. Life, death and rebirth are but one natural cycle. To stop the cycle is to create a stagnant void—the worst possible state. To prevent such a state, the Power has given much.

If the end is upon us, then let it come I say! But let us be remembered for our light, not our darkness! Let us make our end outshine the sun itself! Let us make our end so beautiful as to be worthy of remembrance and . . . sorrow. But most importantly, let our story give others hope that nothing ever ends, it is only transformed.

CHAPTER 1

Rumour on the Sea

I T GLOWED AND GLITTERED with the hue of the sun at its highest point in the sky, before fading to a steady light. Princess Dawn of Algernon clutched the Stone of Desire tightly in her slender hand. "Evan is nearby," she confirmed with a quick nod of her head. "The Stone senses his energy."

"Good. Let's grab that guy and get on with it," Alan responded with his usual impatience. He stood up from where he was kneeling before the fire and dusted his breeches off. "I don't like lingering around here. There is too much—"

"Death?" Mizu interrupted sullenly.

"I was going to say, salt air," Alan covered quickly. Though the bodies had been washed away in a giant tidal wave, the fate of the Glintels still hung heavily in the air, even a full day afterward.

"Nalopa weeps for her children," Mizu whispered, clutching her chest. Her normally bright eyes were red with tears and her lips were parched with sobbing. Everything she had held to be sacred and untouchable had been corrupted. Ralston Radburn's poisonous hand had touched her very heart and left its ugly imprint upon her soul. A terrible anger had been awakened in demure, immortal Mizu. It was an anger that immortals seldom felt.

"He will not get away with it," Ian whispered softly in Mizu's ear and gently touched her shoulder—she did not recoil.

"I know, Ian," Mizu breathed. "He shall pay most dearly for what he has taken. In the end of all things, he shall *pay*." Her fists clenched until her knuckles were white with the strain.

Dawn tried to lighten the atmosphere with a little smile. "Come on, everyone. The Stone says 'north.'"

* * *

Evan's chest ached. There were sharp pains shooting through his ribcage and searing the heart inside. Even in his dreams he could feel the arrows piercing him repeatedly. But more painful than death, was the thought of what he was leaving behind—a woman. A woman for whom he had given everything. A woman for whom he had risked his life and kingdom. A woman for whom he had now given everything. A women who he feared was now left vulnerable and in danger. His soul pulsed with the energy of vengeance.

"Darius."

Evan's eyes fluttered open. He was drenched in a cold sweat and breathing heavily. Above him was a rock ceiling and just a short space down a corridor, sunlight streamed inside. It did not take long for Evan to realize he was in a shallow cavern and he was not alone.

"Kiara," he whispered, seeing the ancient mercenary tending a small fire. *By the Power, this is an awkward situation!* He felt his past life personality of King Darius stirring, yearning to break free. Evan needed all his strength to suppress him.

"I am glad to see you're awake," Kiara said with only a slight hint of emotion. Her keen eyes pierced Evan's. "I found you washed up on the beach last evening. Even when I brought you up here, you did not regain consciousness. I was beginning to wonder if you were still sensible."

Every muscle in Evan's body was tensed. "What do you intend to do now that I am awake? You must know that I have to find my friends and continue our mission. There is absolutely no time to lose." He spoke his words calmly and evenly, attempting to match the steady unruffled pace of Kiara. *I bet she can smell fear.*

Kiara shook her head and gave a little laugh—a laugh that was surprisingly sweet in its way. "Devoted to duty as usual, Darius. Can I never drag you away from your work? No, I suppose not. At least, not by conventional methods."

Evan jumped to his feet and declared firmly, "I am NOT Darius!" He clutched his head as a wave of pain washed over him.

"Say what you will, but I can plainly see the truth," Kiara smiled slightly. "When I look at you, all I see is *him*." Now she stood up and stepped forward, her long garments trailing on the cavern floor. "Give up this useless and dangerous charade. Come with me and be Darius! Let us have what we were denied before! Let us just be a man and woman together, plain and simple. We can do that now, you know. All you need do is walk away from the life of Evan."

Evan felt nauseous and dizzy. *Darius is trying to escape! He feels so strongly about Kiara! It is almost more than I can bear!* Evan stared at the woman before him, as he fought to stay in the present day. He saw her golden flowing hair and pale blue eyes. Yes, the intensity triggered something akin to emotional memories. *She is quite beautiful,* Evan admitted to himself. *And there is something . . . something about her that gives me a familiar warmth . . .* For a moment, his guard began to fall.

"I know it is difficult," Kiara began, coming to stand directly before Evan. "But our love is *so* strong. Surely you can feel it. Surely it can overcome this obstacle. You once told me that our love was forever."

Evan could not help himself and he looked deeply in Kiara's eyes. Her face was so close to his and he could smell a sweet perfume. It was familiar and yet foreign. "Kiara," Evan whispered. A tide of emotion was overwhelming his senses and slowly, the edge of something began to unfold. It was as though the heart of Darius was being revealed to him and something of it was leaking into his own. "He loved you very much," Evan whispered, breathing the sweet air as he spoke.

"He still does," Kiara replied smoothly, bringing her lips before Evan's. "If you let me show you, I am sure you will remember. I am sure you will come to your right mind once again."

Evan felt spelled, for though he knew he should step away, he could not bring himself to actually do it. Some part of him wanted, no, *needed*, to be near Kiara. In a moment, though he did not know how it came to pass, they were sharing a kiss. The moment Kiara's lips touched Evan's, flashes of memory ripped through his mind.

'*The Soul Mirror!*'
'*Do it for me! Do it for us!*'
'*I will leave if you do not try!*'
'*Look what I have given for you!*'
'*Can't you see how I love you?*'
'*I promise you, Kiara. I promise you forever.*'

Evan's eyes moved rapidly under his eyelids as though he were dreaming, but still Kiara continued to kiss him. And then, another image came, but this was of a different woman.

'*Cassandra!*'

'*Evan, you are being poisoned. The scent she uses is a mixture of the Doze Flower and a mountain herb blend which bends the mind and will. She is trying to drive you out and bring Darius in. You have to fight it and remember who you are now. You are not Darius! Not anymore! We are many people in our existence, but we can only be one at a time!*'

"Cassandra!"

Evan's eyes opened and he slowly pushed Kiara away, almost apologetically. "I am sorry, Kiara, but I cannot be the man you want me to be."

The woman did not look surprised. "Someday, you will be," she replied with a slight smile. She did not register shock or disappointment. Her emotions were a mask. "Now I suppose you had better get back to your little friends. They are looking for you."

With these words, there was a slight hint of sadness and without realizing it, Evan found himself saying, "Why don't you join us? Come with us. You seem determined to have revenge on Ralston, so why not do it with us?"

"Darius *is* somewhere inside you," Kiara smiled. "He is worried for my safety."

Evan shook his head quickly. "No, this has nothing to do with Darius's feelings for you. This is my own concern, the concern of Evan."

At this, Kiara revealed some slight shock. "Evan has concern for me?"

"Kiara, you are worthy of the love of the living. You can love and be loved again," Evan replied with his own smile.

Kiara walked to the opening of the cavern and stared out. "You are an interesting man, Evan. I shall be almost sorry to see you go." With that, she leaped out of the cavern and disappeared, leaving Evan much agape about her abilities.

After a moment, Evan got his wits together and stood at the edge of the cavern. It was a rough path down to the beach below. The sea rolled waves onto the rocky coastline, but that was not what Evan's attention was fixed upon. He was staring at two large sailing ships which were floating just off the coast. Several longboats had come ashore and a crew was dining around a fire. With agility of his own, Evan maneuvered his way out of the cavern and crept down amongst the rocks. Something about the situation called for further investigation.

Creeping behind a rather large boulder, Evan was within hearing range of the sailors. *They seem decent fellows,* Evan thought to himself. *Stanbury sailors, unless I miss my mark. They certainly fit the description: huge, fair-haired and having a peculiar sort of accent.*

The sailors were making conversation as they roasted fish upon the open flame. "I have heard the situation in Stanfield has become much worse," said one of the sailors. "They say that King Odin has been deposed and replaced by a small foreign man."

"What's that? A foreigner ruling Stanbury? It cannot be so! King Odin is well-loved!" cried another sailor.

"But haven't you heard the rumours? All the royals in Fadreama are under siege! Seems they were involved in some sort of scheme with that dark southern land, Denzel."

"I don't believe that for one second," another declared. "King Odin would never—"

"It is said there is direct evidence implicating him in the plot. It was brought by the strange dark-haired foreigner."

Evan's heart sped up. *Dark-haired foreigner? Could it be Lance?*

"My sources tell me that the Tower of Fire is now controlled by the foreigner and that the people are serving him without much question. But lately, strange things have been happening and I fear the city itself may be in danger."

"What do you mean, 'strange things?'"

"I don't quite know myself, but word is, evil energy is stirring and it is all centered around the Tower of Fire. I fear the most sacred of grounds is becoming the most corrupt."

"Then you must take us there!" came a young female voice.

From the opposite direction came Dawn, Alan, Mizu and Ian. They approached the sailors slowly and Dawn was smiling brilliantly. Her hair glittered in the sun and she looked very much like a lovely fey vision walking down the beach. "Please, we may be able to help. Can you afford to bear us to Stanfield?"

The sailor who appeared to be in charge stood up. "Greetings, lovely little miss. You and your friends seem to be way off course. No one travels these areas by foot."

"That is why we need your help to get to Stanfield. We can pay," she offered.

The giant blond man tipped his head back and laughed. "No payment necessary, we are going that way ourselves." His blue eyes twinkled and he seemed a goodly sort of man. "My name is Ivor and I am first mate on the vessel *White Rock*. May I have the names of our unexpected passengers?"

Dawn smiled brightly. "I am Dawn, this is Alan, Ian and Mizu. Behind that boulder over there, is Evan. You can see a shock of his bright red hair peeking out."

Evan's lip twitched in embarrassment. *Seems I am not as stealthy as I pretend to be.*

* * *

"So Kiara just left?" Dawn asked Evan, as they sat in a cozy cabin aboard the *White Rock*. The Stanbury sailors were really quite friendly and made no complaint about Dawn and her friends being taken aboard.

"She will never give up on Darius," Evan sighed. "But that is the least of our problems. What do you think is going on in Stanfield? I suspect Ralston has arrived there before us."

Alan nodded quickly. "I heard them mention the 'dark-haired foreigner' and something about a sacred Tower of Fire, whatever that is."

"Things are moving quickly now," Dawn whispered. "I feel time slipping away like grains through an hourglass. I fear that Fadreama is not long for this world."

CHAPTER 2

Legend of the Crystal Points

"**W**HAT ON EARTH IS Ralston doing? Is he honestly pretending to be the King of Stanbury now?" Magica grumbled to herself as she stared into her evil Seeing Water. Her eyes gleamed with malice. "He is supposed to be doing *my* bidding, but lately it seems he is doing whatever he pleases!" The sorceress huffed about her chamber and fingered the glowing Fragment of Cardew attached to a chain about her neck.

"Ralston!" she screamed impatiently into the air and slowly, an image formed.

"My lady, Magica, you bellowed?" Lord Lance de Felda's handsome face materialized in the air. "What is it that you wish, my lady?" There was a smirk hiding just below his visible expression.

"Just what do you think you are doing in that Power-forsaken city of Stanfield?" Magica demanded, hands perched upon her shapely hips.

"My lady, I am gaining ground for you of course," Lance replied smoothly. His voice was really so charming and believable.

"For me? Really? Why do I have so much trouble believing you?" Magica's eyes sparked accusation, but Lance did not react. "What benefit is it to me if you are the King of Stanfield?" she continued on angrily.

"My lady," Lance licked his lips, "have you never heard of the five Crystal Points?"

"No."

"Well then, My Lady, listen and be impressed with my strategy. Soon you will see the benefit."

* * *

The wall surrounding Stanfield City, the capital of Stanbury, was carved directly out of the mountain upon which it sat. Stanfield was practically cradled within the mountain and as such, was well fortified. How it was built no one could recall, for certainly it had been in the beginning of Fadreama.

Dawn and her friends stood before the busy entrance and simply marveled. The ship docks were located outside the city, but it was only a short walk from there to the gates. The group had been on the *White Rock* for a total of three days and so they were more than happy to be upon solid ground again. Now the morning sun shone brightly, giving hope that perhaps things were not as dire as the rumours had led them to believe.

"At all costs, our identities must remain hidden," Evan instructed the others carefully. "We cannot be too cautious in such a city. We obviously look like foreigners, so we will be drawing attention no matter where we go. We have to be on our best behaviour. Alan, I'm looking at you."

"What?" the vampire exclaimed. "I'm not going to blow your cover! My cloak stays on." To emphasize his point, he tightened the clasp at his neck.

"We *all* have to be careful and keep a low profile," Dawn affirmed.

"Well, well, well, if it isn't Princess Dawn and her companions!" came a loud, booming voice from down the road. There, tromping up the mountainous slope, was the platinum-haired spy, Chartreuse. The bells on her dress jangled and the scarves in her hair waved gaudily.

"A low-profile," Ian mused, while Mizu merely covered her face.

"Good morning all!" Chartreuse exclaimed, gliding up the path to meet them. "I'd like to say I didn't expect to see you here, but that would be such a lie—though you are a little earlier than I'd expected. Ivor must have made better time than usual. Typically the *White Rock* is a slower vessel. They make non-timely cargo runs, though it's beyond me how they stay in business." She smiled heartily and said, "I really like Ivor, strong hands you know. What did you think of him?" she asked with a wink.

Alan grimaced at the mental images Chartreuse conjured and exclaimed, "We really don't have time to exchange such banter!"

"Though Alan has a rather crude way of putting it, we do need to get moving, Chartreuse," Dawn corrected delicately. *We hardly have time to be discussing such things!*

"Then I take it you don't want to hear what I know about the goings on in Stanfield?" Chartreuse asked with amusement, knowing full well that they did.

Everyone's ears perked up. Chartreuse was a strange one indeed, sauntering up without a care in the world, yet always well informed.

How she came across her knowledge was less certain, but she was always accurate—at least, according to the psychic, Madame Iris.

"I knew that would get your attention," Chartreuse winked. "And believe me, it's worth a few moments of your precious time."

"Indeed we are in your debt," Dawn coaxed, hoping to appease the spy lest Alan should have offended her.

"Brown-nosing won't get you far with me," she told Dawn lightly. Wetting her full lips, Chartreuse began, "Now listen carefully my honeys. Let me take you back to the beginning, the beginning of Fadreama. When the world was being formed, the gods and goddesses frequented the land more often than they do today. Any place where a divine being enters into the world becomes a truly sacred, holy area. You with me so far?"

The group members nodded, though the sun was rising higher and time was of the essence.

"Five of these sacred areas were selected by the Elemental Spirits, to use as bases for dispensing balance to the world. You can think of them as the rope which binds Fadreama together. The entities of Earth, Air, Fire, Water and Spirit, each selected a base and manifested themselves there."

"Wait!" Alan exclaimed suddenly. "Are you saying that the Elements have consciousness?"

"Why naturally, honey," Chartreuse affirmed. "They think and act of their own free will, though ultimately they serve the will of the Power. But that is not the point here. Over time, these areas of sacredness were incorporated into the human world. Few know the significance of the areas, though their power is sensed by some, but these places have been worshiped for generations. In Stanbury, there is the Tower of Fire for the element Fire. There is the Pool of Water in Marden, the Meadow of Winds in Florian and the Cauldron of the Earth in Bainbridge. The Spirit Gate's location is unknown."

"These places are all off balance?" Evan asked, sensing the Web of Life tremble slightly. He gazed over his shoulder at the city. *We have to hurry!*

"More than off balance," Chartreuse suddenly looked grim. "The Crystal Points, as they are often referred to, have basically turned into magnets for Fragments of Cardew. All Shadow Men, loose fragments and those possessed by humans and demons, have been drawn, or are moving towards, a Crystal Point. They are all gathering and dividing amongst at least four of the points in Fadreama. I won't speak for the Spirit Gate . . . that one is hard to pin down." Chartreuse looked unusually grim.

"That means the Fragments are no longer scattered!" Dawn exclaimed, unsure as to whether she was happy about it or not.

"It also means that if evil gains control of but one Crystal Point, they gain many, many Fragments. The potential for gathering nearly all of them quickly has increased. In one swoop, all Fragments can be absorbed." Chartreuse stared hard at Dawn. *Does this child realize what a precarious situation her world is in?*

"Ralston knows about this, doesn't he?" Dawn whispered, her heart thumping wildly. *A dangerous turn of events . . .*

"Not only Ralston, but Magica too," Chartreuse confirmed. "No doubt you have heard that King Odin has been deposed and a foreigner put in his place?"

"The sailors spoke of this," Evan replied. "So it's true then?"

"Unfortunately," Chartreuse nodded. "And as you may have already guessed, the foreigner is none other than our own Lance— Ralston Radburn. He came to this city with tales to tell using a tongue of honey. A few ominous clouds and thunder claps were all it took to convince the gullible people that the royal family had made a shady deal with the enemy to the south."

"They actually replaced their king with Lance?" Alan was incredulous. "Somehow I find it difficult to believe that Lance is so incredibly likable. He has his charm, but I don't think it can overthrow dynasties which have reigned for generations."

Chartreuse folded her giant arms and smiled. "Ralston is a clever one—don't underestimate him. You seem to forget that he also has Gamren's army of the dead on his side and the Shadow Senshi. All he needs to do is order one of them to attack the city, which scares the people, and then play the hero. Take Verity, for instance."

Ian tensed and his face darkened. *My people . . . My people were so easily deceived and they were not stupid! How could Lance pull such a trick? Surely if he could deceive Verity, then he could deceive Stanfield as well.* "It is easier for Ralston to achieve than we think," he spoke up. "Charisma and an evil tongue can work wonders. Throw in power and there is little hope."

"We have to take him down right now," Mizu asserted angrily. "We attack with all we have and throw him down to the Fallen One!"

"Easy, my dear," Chartreuse warned through her shining lips. "It is dangerous, but there is a way. Though I know not how you will accomplish it and I almost fear what will happen if you succeed." She hesitated and then continued, "You must somehow gain control of the Crystal Points—gain and maintain control of them all. Once you have Fire, Water, Air and Earth, go to Spirit. Just as Ralston would be able to absorb all the Fragments at once by controlling the Crystal Points, you can carry out an all encompassing purification of *Fadreama*."

"The entire world?" Dawn breathed. "At one time evil would be wiped out?"

"Not wiped out, but put back into balance. Essentially you would be re-balancing the elements. I must confess, I do not know what will happen at the time. But I do know this: Fadreama is *dying* and she dies a little more each day. Our naughty friend Ralston is doing everything in his power to preserve the imbalance."

"The only way to defeat Ralston and Magica is to balance the elements?" Evan asked carefully. "Our options seem non-existent. How do you know this?"

"Honey, a good spy never reveals her sources or methods!" The glittering, over-done smile was plastered on Chartreuse's face once again and the grim shadows had fled. "I have told you more than I wanted to, but Dawn's eyes implored me. Now, if you will excuse my hasty exit, I have another engagement." With that, Chartreuse sauntered off in the exact manner she had arrived. Her full hips shook and her bells tinkled as she strode confidently towards Stanfield City.

"Balance the elements . . ." Dawn whispered. "That's what the Three Sisters told us, isn't it?" She fingered the glowing pentacle around her neck. The others did the same.

"They told us alright," Evan affirmed. "But I have no idea how we are going to take over the Crystal Points *and* maintain them. After all, they stretch clear across Fadreama!"

"And Ralston already controls the Tower of Fire," Mizu pointed out. "But we have to find a way! The longer Ralston lives, the more tormented I become!"

"We will find a way," Ian assured Mizu and gently touched her arm.

"Well, one step at a time," Evan clapped his hands. "We need to check out the situation at the Tower of Fire." *My element, according to the Sisters, is Fire. Is this element looking to me for assistance? I think . . . I think I am the only one who can secure this Crystal Point, though I do not know what it will cost me.*

Dawn noticed her cousin's uneasiness and understood, for she felt it within her own heart too. *Even if we succeed, what will our success cost us? What will it cost Fadreama?*

CHAPTER 3

A City in Peril

INSIDE THE WALLS OF Stanfield city was a world created of stone. Everything possible was carved directly from the mountain and the result was a city made of both polished and roughly hewn rock. The elegant and the rugged had combined to form a place unlike any other in Fadreama.

"It is said this city is sometimes called 'The Rock,' for obvious reasons," Ian commented casually, as they traversed a cobbled path. Tall buildings—shops and homes alike—lined the streets, each a mosaic of carefully fitted cut stone.

"I bet it would be terribly cold inside those buildings," Dawn thought out loud with a shiver. "Though Dalton Castle is made of rock, it is nothing compared to this city of stone. I must admit that I have no desire to live in this grey world, as impressive as it is."

"If we are successful, you won't be here long," Alan remarked, while pulling his cloak tightly over his shoulders—hiding the bat wings. To any observer it merely seemed that Alan had an extraordinarily broad, muscular back.

Suddenly, Evan stopped and shielded his eyes from the sun. "You see that point in the distance? I believe that is the Tower of Fire. It looms over everything else." *That place could hold my doom . . .* Inside, Daris stirred restlessly.

"It has to be the Tower," Alan nodded. "We had better—" Alan's words were cut off by the intense ringing of a bell. Soon more urgent bells joined in the deafening racket. Though the notes might have been beautiful if played by gentler hands, there was definitely a shade of violence with this bellman.

"What on earth?" asked Mizu, covering her ears. "It's so loud!"

The bells rang clearly and continuously and the people of Stanfield answered the call. From out of their shops and homes they came, to join those already in the streets. Everyone headed for the path were Dawn and her friends stood in shock. The dazed people then proceeded to make their way quickly down the road, in the direction of the Tower of Fire.

"Those bells must be a summons to the Tower," Evan observed. "I feel . . . something slithering in the Web. Only Ralston slithers and pulls his way along like that! He is nearby and I fear it is he who called!"

"For what purpose, I cannot guess," Ian mused, "though undoubtedly it is a foul one."

"There's only one way to find out," Alan said with a crack of his knuckles. "Let's answer the call."

*   *   *

It was impossible to get lost on the way to the Tower of Fire, for the main road which wound its way through Stanfield, led directly to it. It was as though this one road had been paved for the sole purpose of going to the Tower and that every other use was just incidental.

The Tower of Fire loomed majestically against the bright sky. It was an impressive colour contrast, for the Tower was built using stone with a deep, rusty shade of red. Indeed the Tower looked like a single flame of fire, burning intensely against the blue sky.

Ian whistled lowly under his breath. "Now that is a sight, make no mistake about it." *I must record this in great detail, for I hear a warning in my heart that says much will be lost soon. Things are beginning now—changes—that cannot be stopped.*

"I can feel that this is a holy place," Evan affirmed with a nod of his head. "The energy here is very strong, but something is bending and warping it."

"It's that vile scum, Ralston," Mizu seethed under her breath. "His poison is corrupting this stronghold of the element Fire."

"The people are gathering before that upper balcony," Alan pointed. "I think we're going to see our scum appear very soon. We had better get closer. Come on!"

Evan grabbed Alan's arm. "No, wait. Look at us and look at them. The people here all have fair hair. If we, with our various shades, were to stand amongst them, Ralston would easily be able to pick us out of the crowd. It would be like announcing our whereabouts to him and we don't want to do that just yet. Only Ian here would stand a chance."

"Actually, I think my hair borders more on yellow, while these Stanfield folk are nearly white," Ian pointed out with a lighthearted tone.

Shaking her head, Dawn agreed, "Yes, I think it's better if we stay on the edge of the crowd. That way, if we need to make a quick exit, we can. Who knows what's about to happen." She focused her keen blue eyes upon the Tower balcony. *You're here, Ralston. Show yourself and quit hiding like a coward!*

As though Ralston heard Dawn's inner challenge, he stepped out onto the balcony. A loud cheer erupted through the crowd and hands waved with ecstasy.

"It *is* Lance, just as we thought!" Alan hissed through his vampire teeth.

"Are they actually *cheering* for him?" Mizu was fairly faint with shock. "What *is* going on here?"

Lord Lance de Felda raised his hands to quiet the joyful crowd and nodded with a feigned bashful smile. "Great people of Stanfield, I am honoured by your enthusiastic greeting!" He smiled that charming smile and everyone bought into it.

"This is so wrong . . ." Dawn whispered with wide eyes, as she watched Ralston greet his public.

"My people, my people, listen," Ralston said in Lance's charming tongue. "Disconcerting news has reached my ears and I have called you here out of great concern. Our enemies to the south have been plotting their takeover of Stanbury and they are presently drawing up a plan. We are currently in very great danger from some very sinister foes."

Dawn's heart beat quickly and her blood boiled with anger. *How can he spout such lies? And how can these people honestly buy into it? I admit Lance is charming, but . . . he is lying!*

"Our enemies have entered this fair city," Ralston announced in a high, clear tone. Whispers rippled through the crowd. "But fear not, good people! We can stop them yet, though I require everyone's cooperation! You must all be my eyes and ears! Together, we will weed out these spies and bring them to justice!" Cheers erupted once again.

"You have got to be kidding me!" Alan exclaimed angrily. "He's talking about us, you know."

"Yes, I think we all figured that out," Evan replied tightly. "It's well we stayed out here."

"So now the alarm has been raised and the chances of us getting into the Tower have been made more difficult," Mizu mused with a shake of her head. "We were a little too late." She massaged her temples with a stressful air.

"What I'd like to know," Dawn thought carefully, "is how he knew we were here. Who told him? We've only just arrived!"

"Ralston has spies everywhere," Ian suggested, but trailed off in his hypothesis, when a strange glint caught his eye. A figure in a cloak, just off to their right, was clutching a small dagger. "Evan . . ."

Evan's eyes followed Ian's and he saw the potentially dangerous situation at hand. The figure did not appear very large, which made Evan suspicious. Cautiously, he made his way up beside the slender figure and with lightning fast moves, grasped the wrist which held the weapon. His other arm went around the person's neck and mouth. Like a stealthy assassin, Evan had the figure quickly out of sight, along with his companions. The figure struggled and kicked until the cloak hood fell down, revealing an angry, but very lovely young lady. Her rich blond hair was pulled back into a single braid and her blue eyes shot icy clarity. There was something very noble about her petite features and small, slightly upturned nose. She was very beautiful—perhaps too beautiful for the likes of the large and heavy Stanbury people. Nevertheless, Evan did not release his grip, for the woman still held a sharp weapon.

"Let me go, so help me!" she hissed and then suddenly her eyes opened wide as she gazed at her captors. "Foreigners! You're the ones Lance was just talking about!"

"Indeed we are," Alan said, coming forward with crossed arms. "You going to turn us in?"

The lady's lovely face darkened as though a shadow had passed in front of it. "Not a chance in all the world," she spat. "The day I help that vile, filth of a man, is the day I throw myself into the sea."

Dawn stared hard at the lady—who was only slightly older than herself—and realized that her aura was pure. "Release her, Evan," Dawn stated quickly. "She is no threat to us."

The lady stared back at Dawn with the eyes of one who can truly see. "Who are you?" she asked carefully. "I feel akin to you somehow, as though I should know you—as though we have both shared the same pain."

"My name is Dawn and once, I was called the Princess of Algernon." Even saying such words was painful, for Dawn had banished her old self in a Yule ritual some time ago.

The lady nodded in understanding. "I see now. Yes, we feel the same pain. My name is Sienna and some time ago I was the Princess of Stanbury." She closed her eyes tightly and shivered against a non-existent chill.

"The princess . . ." Ian whispered. "Yes, you have the air of royalty and the grace of a monarch."

"Forget it," Mizu whispered to Ian. "This one looks too clever for the likes of you."

Dawn reached out and took the young lady's hand—the one which did not still clutch a silver blade. Looking into her eyes she said, "I feel your sorrow in this changing world. We are the enemies of a demon called Ralston Radburn—the man you know as Lord Lance de Felda. We have come here to secure the Tower of Fire. Ultimately, we aim to destroy Ralston, as well as all those who serve him."

"Though I only just met you," Sienna began, "for some reason, when I look into your eyes, Dawn, I believe you. But there is something else to be done." She took a deep breath and released it slowly. "I do not pretend to believe that the monarchy will be restored when Lance is gone, for I fear too much damage has been done already for that." She cast her eyes down. "But my family, they must be freed. My father, Odin, my mother Siv, and my three brothers Ottar, Dyre and Einar have been taken prisoner by Lance. I believe they are being held within the Tower. The only reason I escaped was because I was not home at the time of Lance's arrival. He slithered into the city and spun such lies and black magic. I cannot begin to describe my anger!" Her shoulders shook with pent up rage. "How . . . *dare* . . . he!"

"We are all suffering in Fadreama," Dawn replied quietly, "because our world is dying."

Sienna looked down at the dagger in her hand. "Now that I reflect upon it, my plan was poorly concocted and born of pure hatred."

"You were going to attack Lance with that dagger?" Evan asked.

"It was all I could think of doing in my anger," Sienna admitted. "My judgment was clouded but, when I *am* thinking straight, I am not really so naïve." She seemed to have regained her mind and appeared to be quite an intelligent and articulate woman. "For a brief space of time, I lost myself. Thank you for bringing me back from the brink . . . Anger was all I could see and . . . vengeance."

"That I understand," came Mizu, Ian, Alan and Evan's voices all at once.

Sienna stared at them and gave a rueful laugh. "I see Lance has been busy destroying lives everywhere."

"He has been busy for some time," Dawn admitted. "Stanbury was lucky to have survived so long without incident. But this time, Ralston is going for all of Fadreama. This time, everything and everyone is at stake."

"It's more widespread than I had realized," Sienna said and then clenched her fists. "Will you work with me? To throw down Lance? All I want is my family. You can do what you like to the Tower and demon. My business is only to get my family back and to flee with them. I know the secret way into the Tower. I can help you and you can help me." She looked at the group with eager and pleading eyes.

"That is all we can ask of you," Evan agreed, "for our task is not one I would put upon anyone else. We cannot live another's fate, no matter how much we fear our own."

Sienna nodded. "Then let us be gone from here, for it is dangerous. We will return at nightfall."

CHAPTER 4

Sienna, the Wild Child

"**T**HE FOOD OF STANBURY is very heavy, is it not?" Sienna asked Dawn and her companions, as they sat around a wooden table in a local inn.

The spread of food before them did indeed look heavy, for it consisted of fried pork, wide slabs of cheese, dense slices of bread coated in rich butter and large potatoes swimming in thick cream, in addition to several other dishes of the same nature. According to Sienna, such fare was typical in Stanbury—to support their extremely robust frames.

"Sienna, I must say that you do not look very much like the average Stanburian lady. Though you are just as fair in hair colour, you are not so large and . . . bulky," Dawn commented, trying to broach the subject lightly. She stared at the food before her and gently picked away at a potato. She felt heavy just looking at the food.

Sienna laughed a little and took a sip of mead. "I am not a full-blooded Stanburian lady . . . If you can believe it," she smiled a little mysteriously, "my mother is actually from the Cloud Realm."

"Yes! Yes!" Ian exclaimed enthusiastically, jumping to his feet. "I see it in your eyes now! Not the colour, but rather the elegant almond shape—so very lovely and refined." He gave Sienna a charming smile, as Mizu grabbed him by his tunic and pulled him back into his seat.

"Don't wax too poetic on us," Mizu warned Ian with a slightly threatening look.

Sienna, however, seemed to actually be immune to Ian's charms. She merely acknowledged his smile and continued on, "As you can imagine, I have never quite fit in with the Stanburian people, though it never really mattered. For you see, I have three older brothers to inherit the throne. I, therefore, have no obligations to fulfill and can do as I please."

"Sounds fabulous," Dawn sighed. "Some of us have no end to our duties and responsibilities. At one time, I would have given anything to be in your position. Being the heir is more a burden than privilege. So many expectations . . ."

Sienna frowned. "Do not envy me, Dawn. My loneliness and boredom knows no bounds." Her mind seemed to wander into the realms of memory. "Rather than stay in the castle, I would often go to the forest which lies some distance to the north. I would go for weeks at a time and just wander about, living off the land. I must say that I acquired some skill for living in the wild. But what I did not acquire was friends . . . except for Shiva, my owl." She suddenly looked down at her tightly clasped hands. A tear threatened to escape from the corner of her eye, but she willed it back. "Of course, eventually my father will find me a suitable marriage and I will have to abandon my wild ways and try to manage my own household." At this prospect she looked rather grim.

"A wild child of Stanbury, eh?" asked Evan with a slight smile. "You are a very unique young lady and it is well that we stopped you from dooming yourself today."

"A favour I have yet to thank you for," Sienna replied with a faint smile. "Remind me later and I will bestow my proper gratitude." The mysterious manner in which she spoke these words, caused Evan to blush in spite of himself, but before anyone could see, the lights dimmed in the room and candles burst into flame upon a small wooden stage off to the right.

Into the spotlight stepped a large, platinum-haired figure. "Ladies and Gentlemen! My name is Lady Chartreuse and I will be entertaining you this evening!" She shook her shining locks and winked. "Music!" From out of thin air came the exotic sound of a drum and Chartreuse's hips began to sway.

"Now this is something I could have done without," Alan muttered, pushing away his food. "I think I've suddenly lost my appetite."

Evan looked around, amusedly. "The other patrons seem to love it."

"We should try to get into the Tower tonight," Sienna whispered, her voice concealed conveniently by the music. "I know of a secret tunnel which leads directly to the lower levels of the Tower. But we can only access the tunnel from the castle."

"Right," Evan nodded. "Then it is to the castle we must go."

"I must warn you, it will be difficult. Lance has set up surveillance around the castle keep," Sienna explained softly. "Luckily we don't have to actually enter the castle to get to the tunnel. We must merely make it to the outer walls. From there I can direct us to the secret tunnel and we will be well on our way."

"And once we reach the Tower, then what?" asked Mizu with folded arms. "What's our next move? Do we even know how to take control of the place?"

Sienna looked pensive. "There is a way, I think. In the Tower of Fire there is a room which contains but one thing—a single pedestal with a floating orange-red crystal upon it. It is said to be the divine source of power for the Tower. If you can take the crystal—though I must admit I know not if it is possible—then perhaps you can gain control and overthrow Lance."

Evan nodded slowly. "It sounds plausible and highly likely to be true. Didn't you say, Ian, that all tales start with a grain of truth?"

"Precisely," Ian agreed. "Besides, right now we haven't any better ideas." He gave his usual charming smile in spite of the circumstances.

"The crystal must have something to do with the element's spirit," Evan mused carefully. *The Element of Fire is calling out to me, I think. It wishes to be free of Ralston's subjugation. But what can I possibly do to secure the power?*

A voice inside Evan's head seemed to say, 'you will know when the time is right.' *Oh my dear Cassandra, what I wouldn't give to have you with me right now!*

"Let's take a little rest for now," Sienna suggested. "The Innkeeper will become suspicious if we do not go to our rooms. We can leave later when the others have retired for the night. Our window of opportunity is small, but I think we can manage it, somehow, if the Power is with us. You all look very competent." She eyed the group carefully. *So strange these foreigners are. They are all so different and yet travel in the same company. They have endured many things . . . but then, we all have.*

*   *   *

It was well into the night when Dawn heard footsteps marching outside her door. She, Sienna and Mizu were sharing one room, while Alan, Evan and Ian were staying across the hall.

"Someone's out there," Dawn whispered quietly to Sienna, who lay on a small cot by the window. Dawn and Mizu were sharing the rather lumpy bed.

"I think you and your friends have drawn attention to yourselves by simply being foreign. You are easy to spot and after Lance's speech today, people will be on their guard. We have to make our

move now, though I fear we could have quite a rough time of it."
Sienna bit her lower lip in frustration.

"They put us in separate rooms for a reason," Mizu observed,
quickly getting dressed. "I am certain everything was planned from
the moment we walked through the inn door." It had not been the
group's idea to rent two rooms—that had been forced upon them by
the innkeeper, with a muttered speech about decency.

"How will we get word to the others without arousing suspicion?"
wondered Dawn. "I fear there are several people just outside our
door. Can you hear them?"

"I hear them," Sienna said tensely. "Your friends are going to
have to—" she was cut off as Alan burst through the door, though
not of his own power—he had been thrown through the door. He
fell hard into the side of the bed and immediately Dawn was at his
side.

"Alan! Are you okay? What's going on?" Dawn grabbed the
vampire's arm, being careful not to touch his skin.

Alan wiped the blood away from his nose and grumbled, "We're
in trouble."

At that moment, Evan and Ian raced through the door with
several bulky Stanburian guards close behind them. The men looked
positively dangerous by size alone.

"Those are *royal* guards!" Sienna exclaimed with anger.
"Obviously they are working for Lance now! How quickly allegiances
and oaths change!"

"Allegiances and oaths mean nothing!" one man cried. "We are
free to serve whomever we choose! A false king is not acceptable
anymore!"

"Better take a long look at the man in the Tower," Alan muttered,
getting up and grabbing Dawn. "We're going through the window,
so hang on!"

Evan and Ian already had the window open and were throwing
a rope out, when Alan suddenly let out a cry. One of the guards
had cast forth a long leather whip which had wrapped itself firmly
around Alan's neck. In struggling to release it, he dropped Dawn,
who immediately called forth the Light of the Earth. Drawing her
bow, she set her arrow aflame and fired it into the guard's leg, freeing
Alan's now bruised neck.

"Dawn! Alan!" Evan drew his sword, but hesitated to use it.
Cutting the bonds of synergy was such a precarious action. *These are
only men . . . but they are serving Ralston . . . And we must escape!* Darius

urged Evan to use the power, but, as always, Evan resisted. *If Darius advises me to use it, I had better not.* "But I *can* put up a barrier!" With a cry, Evan raised his sword and brought it down with a green streak of light. The group was immediately separated from the guards by a filmy barrier. "It won't hold long," Evan hissed. "Get going! Dawn! Alan!"

Sienna, Ian and Mizu deftly exited through the window and slid down the rope, while Evan urged Dawn and Alan on.

"They're going out the window!" one guard cried. "Shall we go down and intercept them?" he asked the man with the whip, who appeared to be the leader.

The man raised his hand and smile cruelly. "No need. The one we want is still here."

At this, Alan's ears twitched and panic welled up inside him. "Dawn, get out now!"

The guard let out a cry and charged forward, whipping the barrier with such force, that Evan was thrown back against the wall. The barrier crumbled and the guard continued on, though his path was blocked by Alan. Dawn was just lifting her leg over the window ledge when the fight began. Alan drew his crossbow and fired dark energy at the man. Each blow was deftly deflected by the guard's black whip, which cracked through the air like thunder. Without hesitation, he advanced on Alan.

As this was happening, three of the other guards raced to where Dawn was hanging from the window. Her flight had been halted by the sight of her two friends in danger.

"Get out of here, Dawn!" Alan continued to cry. Evan could only look on blurry-eyed. He saw the three huge men grab and restrain his cousin, fling her over their shoulder and march out quickly.

"Dawn!" Alan cried and fired another dark arrow with such malice that it pierced the guard's neck and he crumpled immediately to the ground. Alan now turned to face the others, but before he could draw again, a white shimmering arrow flew through the air, hitting all the remaining men with one shot.

"Sometimes we are forced to take drastic measures," came a voice. Helios extended a hand to Evan and helped him to his feet.

"You fool!" Alan cried, marching towards Helios's hooded figure. "You were here all along and yet you allowed Dawn to be captured! She trusted you!"

"Keep your peace, my friend," Helios responded evenly, though perhaps a little tensely. "Those guards are working for Ralston and he sent them to fetch Dawn. She, therefore, has a head start on us. For Dawn is being taken to the Tower. She has infiltrated Ralston's defenses and now only waits for backup. That girl can hold her own until we arrive, trust me. But come now, she cannot wait forever! We must get to that tunnel!"

CHAPTER 5

Underwater Passage

DAWN AWOKE TO FIND herself in a most comfortable and tastefully decorated room. *This can't be that horrid inn . . .* She opened her eyes wider and observed the spacious room, with its large hearth and merrily burning flames. Her bed had ample pillows and blankets, creating something of a protective nest. Aside from the usual bedchamber items, there was a beautiful circular table with a high backed chair and a luxurious spread of food— Algernonian food.

Placing one hand on her forehead, Dawn sat up and swung her legs over the edge of the bed. *That's right . . . I was captured by Ralston's guards. So where am I now? This is hardly a prison cell! Did they knock me out? I don't remember what happened after they took me from the inn . . .*

A soft knock at the door interrupted her thoughts. "Your Highness?" It was a young man's voice. "Lord Lance wishes your presence in the Crystal Chamber. But first, he bids you to satisfy your hunger and to refresh yourself with a bath. He told me to tell you that hard travel does not become you . . . And that you have become most . . . er . . . careworn. You are a princess and must present yourself as such. And . . . Lord Lance says you must purify yourself before entering the Crystal Chamber. He said it is very important." The man's voice shook a little with the effort of relaying such an impudent message.

At the mention of 'princess,' Dawn cringed. Yet as much as she wished to tell the man beyond the door to go away, she shook her head defiantly. *If Ralston wants to meet with Princess Dawn, then so be it! Purify myself? Ha! It is time for him to know that* this *princess is through being trifled with! I will accept his hospitality, if only to show I am not afraid! After all, I am Alice Light's daughter! The child of a Goddess! If it is a princess he wants, then it is a princess he shall get!* Though Dawn had hated being viewed as such in the past, at this moment she embraced the title and the strength which came with it. *I will speak for all those who cannot!*

Sliding out of the soft bed, she caught a look at herself in the mirror and thought with shock, *I do look careworn . . . I have seen far too much.*

"Princess?" came the young male voice beyond the door again. "Is everything quite alright? I am sorry if I offended you, but those were Lord Lance's words, not mine."

Things haven't been alright for a long time, she thought ruefully, yet replied, "Tell his lordship I will be ready shortly." Dawn's brow was creased in a combination of determination and defiance. *I will make you proud Mother. I will not kneel to him.*

*   *   *

King Odin's castle loomed over the rocky land with decided majesty. The sun was just rising behind it, giving the impression of a glowing aura about the walls.

"My home," Sienna muttered bitterly, "for all it's worth now."

"A home is people, not a place," Evan said, approaching her from behind. "Now, where is this tunnel you spoke of? You said we do not have to enter the castle itself?"

"Yes, that's right. There's a secret entrance where the moat meets the waterfall which feeds it. Behind it is a pool which we will have to swim through. There are various air pockets along the way—you can all swim I hope?"

"Like a fish," Mizu replied with a slightly ironic undertone.

"She means we will manage," Ian spoke up with a smile. "In any case, it is safer than our more direct options. I think it would be best if we avoided confrontations for the time being." Ian was thinking of his own lack of skills as far as physical combat was concerned.

"Speak for yourself," Alan muttered touching his bow.

"Alan, he enjoys a good fight," Helios explained from behind his mysterious cloak. "Fighting to protect a loved one is one thing, but for vengeance . . . it involves a different mindset. If vengeance is in your heart, you must be prepared to deal with the consequences." With this said, Helios lapsed into a pensive silence.

Sienna raised an eyebrow. She sensed a certain tension since Helios had joined the group. *He has been through much too . . .* Shaking her head she said, "This way." *Can he see my mind? Vengeance is my cause . . .*

Sienna led the group stealthily over the stony terrain towards the castle. As it was still quite early, there was not a soul about. The moat which surrounded the grand structure did indeed originate from a waterfall on the far northern side of the castle. "That's the place,"

Sienna affirmed. The spray from the waterfall was cold, but not frigidly so—it would be okay to swim. Placing her back against the stony cliff, Sienna began to sidestep her way along a very narrow ledge.

"Behind the falls?" Evan asked while following suit. The others came behind him.

"Yes, just a little distance," Sienna replied, vaguely able to make out the opening behind the falls in the early light. "I have been here before, so trust me." *Been here to cry alone, that is.* "You have to jump a little distance, so be careful you don't slip."

"Forget jumping," Alan exclaimed, revealing his bat wings and hovering before the falls. With total ambivalence towards the others, he proceeded to fly behind the falls.

Ian laughed good-naturedly. "We wouldn't have him any other way."

Sienna just shook her head and helped the others make the short jump behind the falls.

*   *   *

"Ralston may be on the right track with the Crystal Points," Magica began as she paced about her throne room, "but I hardly think he is working for *my* benefit!" She clenched her fists and continued to address the unfinished being she was piecing together using Fragments of Cardew. "He thinks me a fool! Well, I see through his little ploy. He works only to advance himself. Typical demon! Of course, I work only to advance myself as well." An evil smile curled her lips. "This Fragment about my neck has increased my powers ten-fold! It is time to utilize it fully!" She held the Fragment in her hands tightly. *It is time to use Ralston against himself! There can only be one of us in control of this battle . . .*

A dark light shone from the Fragment and a casual observer might have believed she was absorbing it into her soul. However, the sorceress now turned and faced her unfinished being. Laying the Fragment upon it, she began to release it and chant, "The time has come, my darling! Feel the breath of life! We needn't use Dawn's energy to animate you when we have Ralston's, the most powerful demon there ever was! Use his power! Live!"

The handsome man before her convulsed violently, drew in a sharp breath and stretched out his arms. Magica laughed. "You're alive!"

The man gave a half-smile and suddenly grabbed Magica by the throat. "W . . . What are you doing, you fool? I c . . . c . . . created you!" she choked under his grip. "I . . . am . . . your mother . . ." A look of sheer terror now filled Magica's eyes—something she rarely, if ever, showed. It was in this brief moment that she realized how Alice must have felt when darkness had covered Devona. Such a short space of time, such a large revelation. Magica knew without a doubt that this was her last second on earth—a second that was filled with betrayal and something akin to remorse. *Alice . . .*

Magica's creation pulled her close against his body and there was a blinding flash of light. The man laughed in a rich voice that echoed off the wall of Magica's castle.

"You!" came a voice from the arched doorway. There stood Kane, breathing heavily with his sword drawn. His eyes blazed with anger and genuine loss. For all his evil ways, Kane had loved Magica. She had been his whole world and now there was nothing. With a terrific yell, he charged towards the Creature.

Then, the Creature began to speak in a voice only Kane could hear. Kane stopped short in his death charge, a look of shock playing across his features. Suddenly he dropped his sword to the stone floor with a clatter. Falling to one knee and clutching his head, Kane screamed, "No! It's not true!"

The Creature nodded calmly, eyes glinting. With one last scream of torment, poor Kane jumped to his feet and ran screaming out onto Magica's balcony. The waves crashing on the shore below covered any sound Kane made when he hurled himself into the sea.

Again, the Creature laughed. "I am coming, Lord Ralston."

*   *   *

With one shapely and elegant hand, Sienna indicated towards a tiny pool of water, located on the floor of the cave. Outside, the sound of the falls was deafening and the water droplets glowed in the rising sunlight.

"This pool is the entrance to a long tunnel which passes through the lower levels of the Tower. There is a slight chance that we can enter unnoticed, though I am certain Lord Lance's henchmen have never taken their eyes off us."

Evan nodded slowly. *Sienna is very astute and not a fool, make no mistake about that. She is like Cassandra in that she knows danger and yet makes no attempt to avoid it—she merely accepts it.* "Well, let's waste no more time chatting. Dawn needs us."

"Have a little more faith in her staying power," Helios spoke up. "You all underestimate the strength of Dawn's personality."

"As if you know anything of Dawn's personality," Alan muttered angrily, rolling up his tunic sleeves. "Let's just go!"

Sienna nodded. "There are air pockets along the way. Follow my lead and you will not miss them." With that, she kneeled down before the pool and gently rolled forward into the water without so much as a ripple. The others followed suit as the sun rose higher against a blood red sky.

*   *   *

"Her Royal Highness, Princess Dawn of Algernon," announced a burly herald. Dawn stood under the stone arch which led into the Crystal Chamber of the Tower. She was freshly bathed, perfumed and dressed like royalty. It was clear to everyone that this was a young lady of pure royal blood (much different than the bedraggled child the guards had brought in only hours earlier). Once cleaned up, Dawn looked entrancingly beautiful. Toil and danger seemed to have given her years of maturity far beyond her true age. All the guards and courtiers in the room could not help but feel a sense of awe. She held her head high and straight using poise she never realized she had.

The Crystal Chamber was obviously set up like a throne room, though it was more comfortably furnished with tables, sitting areas, plants and decorative tapestries. Red candles burned softly upon an alter in the southern area of the room—a tribute to the element, Fire, which controlled this Crystal Point.

Dawn did not deny her royal announcement. *Though I banished it, perhaps it is not my destiny to escape it. Perhaps I must be more accepting of basic truths. There is power in my title and I shall begin earning back the right to bear it!* "I am Princess Dawn of Algernon and *this*," she cried pointing a finger, "is an abomination! Where is the royal family? I will only deal with the rulers of Stanbury, not some impudent usurper!" Her face blazed defiance.

"They are not your concern." Lord Lance—Ralston—stepped forward, handsome and charismatic as ever. Everyone but Dawn bowed respectfully.

Traitors, the lot of them! Dawn thought.

"My dear girl—young lady, I should say, for that is what you have truly become," Lance began charmingly, "you look positively radiant." He came before Dawn and smiled eerily. Gently he reached out and traced his fingers along her cheek. "My sweetest cousin, I have brought you here to help me." His eyes fixated on hers and the smile did not waver from his face. Somehow, Dawn knew she was not being offered a choice.

CHAPTER 6

Fire Speaks

"**Y**OU HAVE FALLEN VERY low indeed," Dawn replied, trying to keep her voice steady and level. "Demanding help from me? This is a dark day for you, isn't it?" Immediately she saw her words strike a note of truth, for Lance's smile flickered and his eyes sparked for an instant. However, he did not give away his façade to the brainwashed onlookers.

"We are family, my dear," Lance smiled through his pearly white teeth. "In times of crisis, family comes together. I would have asked your mother, but, alas, she is unavailable." Now it was Ralston's turn to gloat in the unrest he caused within the rigid young lady before him. *She has changed, this princess. She is stronger and, perhaps, more dangerous. I mustn't underestimate her. She may yet be the undoing of us all—evil and good.*

"Family!" Dawn scoffed. It was the only word she could utter, so great was her anger. *How dare he bring my poor mother into this! She, who has given everything for this doomed world!*

"But enough of this small talk," Lance continued, offering his arm to Dawn, who had no choice but to take it. Purposefully he led her to the center of the room. There was a smooth stone pedestal, with something hovering just above its surface, draped in a silken black cloth. With one sweep of his free hand, Lance uncovered the mysterious object. A glowing red crystal floated motionlessly in the air above the pedestal. It radiated with a fire that was so deep, so intense, that no earthly words could describe it. This was Fire in its most concentrated, pure form. The very spirit of the element was housed within this crystal.

The element of Fire's Crystal Point! Dawn thought. *This crystal is Fire's connection to our world! Should anything . . . or anyone, do this crystal harm, chaos would reign! The elements would become so off balance . . . even more so than they already are!* She looked at Lance out of the corner of her eye. *What does he mean by showing me this? Here he is within the Tower of Fire and yet it seems he does not have control over the element. Could it be he . . . cannot . . . gain control over this crystal? Perhaps he thinks I can?*

"I know what you are thinking, cousin," Lord Lance said smoothly. "Why do I not use this crystal to my advantage? Well, it is as you guessed; I cannot manipulate it." This last phrase was spoken in a much quieter voice, as though he was trying to hide some sort of twisted shame. "You, however, are the daughter of a goddess and have power in your own right, Dawn. There is no choice in this matter, so do not attempt to argue. I want you to manipulate this crystal and confer its powers onto me."

Dawn could not help but give a laugh. "You honestly think, even if I could control this crystal, that I would ever, ever, dream of conferring this power onto you? In what world would I do such a thing?"

Lance leaned in close, so that his icy eyes could penetrate into Dawn's. Deep within the blue eyes of Lance, Dawn could see the hideous being who was controlling her cousin's body. She did not, however, avert her gaze. Instead, she returned his stare unwaveringly.

"You have no choice," Lance seethed. "If you care anything at all about your friends, who are now racing here to rescue you, or about your family trapped in Devona, you will do exactly as I command. Even without the power of Fire, I could destroy everyone you love in an instant. Do not test me. Do not toy with me. I have been at this for far too long. I have no mercy, no remorse, no regret. I am not like you. I have no soul and so I am bound to no one."

"You forget quickly, Ralston," Dawn replied, desperately fighting to keep her voice level. "You sold your soul, long ago, to the Fallen One. He is your master and you can never be rid of him. Fail and he will torment you for all eternity."

Dawn's words echoed off the stone walls and resonated within Ralston's consciousness. He grabbed her by the sleeve of her dress and pulled her violently close. He extended his free hand into the air and a dark cloud materialized. Within the cloud, Dawn could see her friends swimming the underground channel towards the Tower. She could also see an air pocket which they were approaching steadily. *They mean to catch their breath,* she thought. Ralston twisted his hand and the air pocket began to shrink in size, just as her friends approached it. Sienna led the way up and a shocked look passed across her face, as she realized the air was not where it should be. Panic immediately showed on the faces of her companions.

"No!" Dawn screamed, losing her composure. "They will die!"

"Manipulate the Fire Crystal for me and I will let them live awhile longer," Ralston replied easily. "It is your choice, but you will have to make it quickly."

There was no time for Dawn to weigh the pros and cons of the situation. There was no time to offer an alternative or even think up a plan. Her friends would be dead in seconds if she did not agree to help her enemy. "Yes! For the Power's sake! I will do whatever you ask, just give them air!"

"I will give them more than that," Ralston laughed. "I will make their journey easier." With that, the water in the underground tunnel completely disappeared, leaving Dawn's companions gasping and looking very confused. Ralston immediately dismissed the dark cloud and returned his full attention to Dawn.

"You see, they are alive and will be arriving here soon. Now, hold up your end of the bargain. The Fire Crystal." He nudged her towards the blood red light and stepped back.

Dawn's face glowed red with the reflected light. She could feel a heat coming off of it, much stronger than anything she could produce with her very own elf Fire Stone. This was pure, raw and untamed Fire. *How am I to do this? It feels so very wrong . . .* Dawn reached out her hands and held them on either side of the stone without actually touching it. She closed her eyes and tried to focus on the power before her. Lance leaned forward eagerly, eerie shadows flickering off of his face.

The minutes ticked by and yet nothing happened. Dawn focused all she could, but there was no energy exchange. She felt absolutely nothing. *Perhaps it is not I who is destined to hold Fire. Perhaps I cannot hold fire . . .* "Nothing is happening," she told Ralston. "I don't think I *can* do it. I don't understand it, but I honestly feel nothing!"

Lance had to consciously keep his jaw from falling open. *How can this goddess child . . . This holder of an elfin weapon . . . This creator of Crystal Children . . . This purifier of evil . . .*

"I do not understand it myself," Dawn continued. "I think it is not my destiny."

Lance was absolutely taken aback. He had never even considered that Dawn may not be able to manipulate the Fire Crystal. And yet, he knew, someone could. *Perhaps one of her companions . . . We shall try them all on for size and if none can do it, they all shall perish here together.*

A guard approached Lance from the doorway. "My Lord, there are intruders in the building. They are on the lower levels. Do you want them eliminated or captured?"

"Let them come at their own pace, but make sure they are led here. I want them calm and uninjured," Lance instructed, as a conflicted grin spread over his face. *Yes, one of her companions may hold the power I seek. I sense the stones trembling now, as if some great force were waiting to be unleashed.*

* * *

"Up these stairs, quietly," Sienna whispered, brushing a strand of hair from her face.

"Why up?" asked Alan, his eyes darting around suspiciously.

"Because all the other ways are blocked, that's why," Sienna sighed in frustration. "I have no idea where my family is being held, but we have to start somewhere."

"I don't like the energy in this place," Mizu breathed. "It feels hot and dry . . . This is no place for Water and—Evan? Are you okay?"

Evan's skin was flushed with vibrant energy and his red hair seemed to blaze now more than ever. Faint outlines of freckles appeared, but were delicate on his smooth Alexandrian skin. "There is . . . something about this place," he breathed heavily. "The power is so strong, I can hardly see straight. Can't you all feel it?"

"Evan . . ." Ian touched his friend's back, "though we feel something, I don't think any of us are feeling what you are."

"The Three Sisters granted you charge over an element, Evan." It was Helios who spoke from beneath his shroud. "You are connected spiritually to Fire, correct?" Evan nodded, his interest aroused. "Then it makes sense that the stronghold of Fire would affect you more than anyone else. And be this a trap or no—I think it likely is—we have no choice but to press onwards through the open doors. Wherever it leads us, so be it. That is where we must go."

"Come on then," Sienna pressed. "Up these stairs, now!"

And so they climbed around the twisted staircase, knowing full well they were likely walking into a trap. However, trap or no trap, Dawn was in danger and not one among them would leave her in Ralston's clutches. Alan's fists were clenched tightly and his brow showed signs of a nervous sweat.

* * *

"They are here," Lance said tightly, just as Dawn's friends burst through the only door to the round Crystal Chamber. The group stopped short when they saw Lance standing in the center of the room with a rather beautiful looking Dawn by his side. Their faces were illuminated red by the power of the Fire Crystal which suddenly flared and pulsed.

"At last we are all here," Lance exclaimed in a dark tone. "I have very little patience left. Your *precious* Dawn here, cannot command the Fire Crystal. I will have its power conferred onto me, so which one of you can do it? Do not think to disobey me, because I will kill Dawn in an instant if you do." His voice was cold and held hard truth.

From the moment Evan had entered the chamber, he had been unable to move his body. It was as though he were no longer in control, yet it was somehow different than when Darius took over, for Evan retained his mind at this moment. Now, as Lance spoke his threatening words, Evan felt a surge of powerful heat moving through his body and . . . an anger. Such an anger! He could not contain the feelings and suddenly found himself screaming something similar to Dawn's earlier exclamation, "THIS IS AN ABONMINATION!"

Everyone jumped at the voice, which although was undoubtedly Evan's, was laced with something primal, otherworldly . . . elemental. Evan stepped forward and began to glow with red light, as though his entire body were a burning ember. His cloak fell away and his fairy wings appeared, glittering with veins of iridescent light.

"This is an abomination!" he repeated. The pendant around Evan's neck, which had been given to him by the Three Sisters, was pulsating orange, casting alternating shadows on the tower walls. The light seemed to connect Evan directly to the Fire Crystal.

Ralston was in delighted shock. *This boy is the key to the Fire Element! I must have his power!* From his tunic, Lance produced a Fragment of Cardew. *If I can but implant this precious thing inside the boy, he will be mine to control.* Tossing Dawn roughly to the side, Lance approached Evan warily.

Evan pulsed brighter, as if sensing the threat. "LISTEN!" he roared. "I am FIRE—the deep heated flame and desire in all things. I am the drive of passion and the rage of action. I am that which burns and destroys to bring about new life. I will burn away all that is evil. The Air will fuel me, the Water will cleanse away the debris and the Earth will rise again. This is what is coming. You would be wise to heed this warning now, for you will not realize it is here, until it is over!"

Dawn's eyes grew wide and her soul felt cold with magical energy, despite the flames about her. This was a prophecy if she ever heard one and somewhere deep within the core of her being, she knew it would come to pass. What part they would all have to play out in the drama, she did not yet know.

Now Evan's head tipped back and a beam of red light shot out from the center of his forehead—his 'third eye' chakra, one of the seven energy points in the body. This beam of light connected with the Fire Crystal and the light emitted was nearly blinding.

"I am no longer safe housed in this man-made structure," Evan declared. "For these end times, I shall move freely as a human body, so that I may be there for the final hour. My counterparts Earth, Air and Water, you too will be as I am. For we, the Elementals of the Lady and Lord, know what the Power has in store for this world. And what's more, we know the Element SPIRIT!"

Mizu's forehead emitted a blue light, while at the same time Alan's shone green and Ian's yellow.

Lance pursed his lips tightly. He did not like where this was going. *There is practically no way I can get close enough to force this Fragment of Cardew into the boy. And I do not like the energy being emitted by his companions. Oddly enough, Dawn is doing nothing. Where is her great energy? I had best desert this place and move on to the next Crystal Point. Perhaps I can do something of consequence there . . . before these oddities do!* Slowly he began to make for the hidden door in the far wall of the tower. All of the other occupants of the room appeared frozen in time.

"This sacred tower has been defiled by evil! It screams for purification! When all the Crystal Points are in alignment, the purification process can begin! Until then, let this tower be returned to the elements!" Evan cried, as a great 'whoosh' of flame sprang up all around. The Fire Crystal pulsed and disappeared, as Evan grew brighter and merged with it. All around, the flames roared.

CHAPTER 7

Feelings Revealed

KIARA STOOD ON A small rocky hill, just outside the Tower of Fire. Her keen eyes were fixed upon the burning monument as she gripped her bow tightly. *Darius . . .* she thought. *Evan . . . Is there no end to what you are? How many facets do you have? Like a cut jewel, you have so many different faces. It makes me wonder, am I worthy of even one of them? Perhaps, as I always feared back then, I am reaching too high and beyond my own sphere.* Kiara's knuckles went white with tension. *And yet I love him still, whether or not I should. Darius . . . I honestly do love him and I would give all that I am just to be with him again, be it in life or death.*

"I, too, know what it is like to love someone completely and yet have that love lie beyond my reach," an enchanting voice spoke from behind Kiara.

"Chartreuse," Kiara murmured without turning around. "These are difficult times we find ourselves in."

The exotic dancer came to stand beside Kiara, her bells and robes fluttering in the wind. "Everyone thinks such things in their time. They all believe they are witnessing the end."

"Only this time we are right," Kiara replied softly. Her eyes did not tear up, though her voice sounded pained.

"When a Crystal Point is destroyed, we have powerful evidence that the end is coming. Yes, I dare say it is this time. Somehow, I never expected it to come at all. I always thought the Crystal Points would be spared but . . . can you feel it?" Chartreuse held her face high into the smoky breeze. "The energy of the falling point is dissipating. The Fragments of Cardew that were attracted to this site are now wandering off again . . . to await the purification that is to come." She paused. "I am inclined to believe in Dawn. If she is given the chance, I really do think she can cleanse this world for good. Someday, we will be rid of those dirty Fragments altogether! It is a comforting thought, I suppose." Chartreuse lapsed into pensive silence.

A cold wind blew by and Kiara clutched her chest. *A neutral Fragment lies within me . . . In the end, what will become of me? Am I fighting a losing battle?*

*   *   *

The same cold wind which had chilled Kiara and Chartreuse, now tousled the long brown hair of the Heart Temple's high priestess, Lily. She was standing in the gardens just outside of the main Temple. The icy wind chilled her very soul and she narrowed her eyes as she stared up at the sky. *I feel that the revolution is near . . . We must make ready . . .*

"My Lady?" asked Priestess Andrea, sister of Alice's husband, King Alexander.

Lily broke her reverie and came to Andrea's side. Putting her hands on the woman's shoulders she said, "Do you feel it? We have lost one of the Elemental's protection. Fire has abandoned Fadreama."

Andrea nodded slowly. "I knew something had happened, that is why I sought you out. I fear . . . I fear that is not all we have lost." Andrea bit her lip and fought back tears. "Alice . . . she is fading . . . Is there anything we can do to help her?"

Lily's entire body felt cold and she thought, *I am getting too old for this heartache.* "I'm afraid that Alice is on her own now, if 'Alice' still exists at all. I suspect Syoho must have taken over completely by now."

"If a Goddess cannot save our world, what chance do we have?" Andrea asked in a hopeless voice.

Putting on a brave face Lily replied, "Take heart, Andrea. We are only forsaken if we give up. Now, rally the girls and ladies together. We have a journey to make!"

Andrea nodded and turned to go, but Lily had one more order, "And summon Boudicca!"

*   *   *

"No! We cannot leave yet! We have to find my family!" Sienna screamed in hysterics. The waves of heat from the burning inferno made breathing difficult. "I am not leaving without them!" she coughed.

"We can't just go blundering about here!" Alan cried out furiously. One arm was wrapped protectively around Dawn. He looked as though he were about to sweep her up into his arms and escape through one of the windows high up in the tower.

Mizu raised her arms over her head and declared bravely, "I shall try to quell these flames with Water. Dawn, please help me with your Water Stone! We can save what is left of this sorry place!"

"No!" Evan cried fiercely. "This Tower must return to the Earth. It must be destroyed!" With these words said, Evan's knees buckled and he crumpled to the ground in a dead faint.

"Evan!" Dawn screamed, rushing to her cousin's side. She picked up his limp hand and held it gently, feeling for a pulse. "He's alive, but we must all get out of this place!"

"What of the fire?" Ian asked with a cough.

"We should obey Evan's wish in that matter," Dawn replied firmly. "He is the Fire and we have to respect the Element."

"Look! I don't care about respect right now!" Alan exclaimed angrily. "We need to leave!"

"Not without my family," Sienna demanded firmly. "I helped you get here, now you must help me. It is a bargain!" Tears streamed down her sooty face. "I will curse you all for eternity if you do not help me find them!" Her voice was desperate.

At last, Helios spoke, "We cannot risk Princess Dawn," he declared firmly. "I refuse to put your family above her, Sienna." His words seemed strangely hard. "We all lose things. We all sacrifice in these dangerous times." His voice then softened slightly and he continued, "However, we did have something of a bargain." Helios lifted Evan up off the ground and held the unconscious fairy prince, while standing protectively close to Dawn. "Alan, you are the most resilient of us all with your vampire powers. Find Sienna's family, if they truly are in this place. Use that dark power of yours to smell their blood or whatever it is that you do. Find them and bring them outside, if you can."

These words hung in the air precariously, as the fire raged more dangerously. Alan stared wordlessly at Helios and then at Dawn. The princess looked conflicted, but at last said softly, "You *are* the strongest."

His eyes darkened and he turned away. "Get out of here, now. The smoke is too thick for your *human* lungs."

"Alan . . ." Dawn said, but Helios was already pushing her out the door. Mizu and Ian were right behind him.

Sienna looked at Alan pleadingly and said, "Tell me they are alive?"

*   *   *

The Tower of Fire raged and glowed blood-red against the noon sky. Dawn and the others stood some distance away, anxiously waiting for Alan to return. "We shouldn't have left him," Dawn whispered worriedly. "We should have forced Sienna to accept the facts—her family is dead. Ralston would never suffer to keep them alive. They would have posed too much of a threat. He wanted the people of Stanbury under his complete control. To leave the royal family around would present too much of a temptation for the fools who remained loyal to them." Dawn's words were cold and empty. She was angry. Yes, *very* angry. Someone she cared about deeply was being needlessly put at risk. *Yes I feel sorry for Sienna, but like Helios said, we all have lost things. We cannot put what we have left at stake.* Dawn was surprised by her own lack of empathy. She had indeed seen too much and lost too much. It had hardened her and this frightened her.

Mizu put a comforting hand on Dawn's shoulder. "Alan is very strong. If Sienna's family is alive, he will bring them out safely. If they are gone, he and Sienna will come back alive."

"She's right," Ian agreed. "Alan is far too stubborn to die in a simple fire."

"This is no simple fire." It was Evan who spoke. His eyelids fluttered open and he lifted himself up onto one elbow on the ground where Helios had laid him. "This is the Fire of Fire. This flame cannot be quenched. It will burn until its task is complete and the Tower is nothing but ashes. Everything that is within will be reduced to cinder." He looked pale and unsteady. "I felt that power. I feel it within my heart still. There is a burning . . . not painful, but rather, powerful. I am changed, somehow."

"You have taken the spirit of Fire within you," Helios nodded. "You house a very raw power. When the time comes, I know not what will become of you."

Evan pursed his lips together tightly. "In all honesty, I don't think it really matters at this point, so long as I can do some good in this lost world." He then closed his eyes and slipped back into unconsciousness.

Mizu gently felt Evan's forehead. "He has a terrible fever," she whispered and trickled some cool water upon his brow.

"What can we do for him?" Dawn fretted, glancing nervously between Evan and the unsteady Tower.

"We must let the Fire run its course through his body. Evan will adjust to Fire's power. It is his destiny, so it cannot be any other way,"

Helios explained with a soft note in his voice. He knew something of sacrifice and destiny—it saddened him to his very core.

Dawn stared hard at Helios's hooded figure for a moment. *What secrets and sorrows do you carry by yourself? What burdens do you bear that you cannot share with us? You are indeed our ally, wise and true, but I know next to nothing about you, Helios.* Helios caught Dawn staring at him and she quickly turned away. *Alan . . .*

The great Tower of Fire was shaking unsteadily now. "It won't hold up much longer," Ian observed. The loud squawking of water fowl could be heard overhead from somewhere behind the gathering clouds. A song drifted through his mind:

Embers from the sky a falling, hark the waters birds are calling. Then the winds will cease to blow and nothing from the Earth shall grow. When the great light comes to pass, Fadreama shall find peace at last.

Ian drew a sharp breath and clenched his fists.

A tremendous rumbling spread across the ground like an earthquake. The Tower of Fire swayed slightly and then started to implode upon itself, coming down . . . down . . . down . . . ashes blowing in the wind and mixing with the dust upon the earth.

"No!" Dawn screamed. "Alan!" The Tower was down and a light rain began to fall, sending hisses of steam upward from the rubble. Tears streamed down Dawn's face and she turned to Helios suddenly in anger. "*You* are the one who told him to help Sienna! You knew her cause was a lost one and yet you still left Alan behind! How . . . how could you?" Her last words were nearly a whisper and her eyes were filled with the sadness of betrayal.

Helios did not respond but merely pointed behind her. A figure was making his way across the rubble towards them. He was covered in a fine layer of ash, but there was no mistaking the bat wings.

"Alan!" Dawn screamed, racing towards him. She did not hesitate to throw her arms around the young man and hold on tightly. "I was so worried," she whispered into his chest.

Seemingly stunned, Alan did not respond for a moment. Then, slowly he wrapped his arms around Dawn and held her close. "As if I would die and let Ralston continue unhindered. I have not yet had my revenge."

Dawn looked up into Alan's eyes and blinked back the tears. "You can never leave me, do you understand?"

"I . . ." Alan was not sure how to respond to these sudden emotion-filled words.

"Please," Dawn pleaded, "you cannot leave me alone. Do you see now?" The world seemed to stop for an instant, as though Dawn had used the Stone of Time to halt everything. Dawn looked up into Alan's eyes with pure sincerity and said very clearly, "I love you." The words flowed out so easily, so naturally. Nothing was forced. It was as though the obvious had at last been stated, as though the feelings which had always been there were finally given a voice.

And Alan, the tormented and detached, cursed young man, replied, "I will never leave you, Dawn. I promise." And he did not feel any pain from her skin's soft touch—only . . . warmth.

CHAPTER 8

The Priestess and The Prince

EVAN WAS DREAMING. HE was standing in a very dark place. It was exceedingly dry, not unlike a desert. A hot wind drifted in and out like a tide, soundlessly ruffling his hair. Suddenly, out of nowhere, a campfire appeared and blazed brightly. Evan found himself walking towards the roaring light, in spite of the intense heat. Sitting on a log beside the fire was a man wearing a golden crown and draped in robes of yellow, orange and red. The folds of cloth seemed to be made of fire itself, for they danced and flickered with a life of their own.

"Who are you?" Evan asked, finding his voice at last. His throat felt terribly dry and parched.

The rather large, handsome man looked up, but did not smile. His hair was red like Evan's and his face was an illuminating ruddy hue. "I am the King of Fire, Djinn." As he spoke these words, the ground glowed brightly, like the embers of a fire. The earth trembled and in the distance Evan could see a great volcano spewing forth molten hot lava.

"And you, Evan, are my guardian on this earthly plane. You carry me within you and shall do so until the other elements are freed. Then, the great purification will begin." Dijinn stared intensely at Evan, who was unable to speak freely. The King walked up to the fairy and each time his foot made contact with the ground, he left a glowing footprint. "The time of Fadreama is over," Dijinn said sternly.

Evan wanted to call out and step back. He could feel the fire burning so hot, that he fearing turning to ashes himself.

"This is your destiny," Dijinn continued. "You must not fail."

And then, like a cool refreshing breeze, another voice spoke, "Evan." He could feel the gentle calmness of the voice and craned his neck to see the speaker. "Evan," the voice said again and began to chant,

"Illuminate like the FIRE,
But don't burn like the blaze.
For who can see anything,
Through the smoke and the haze?"

Evan's eyes opened. It was nighttime and he could see the stars twinkling overhead. Something cool was being held on his forehead—a hand. "C . . . Cassandra . . ." he murmured.

The priestess Cassandra smiled down upon Evan, with glassy eyes. "Yes, Evan. I am here. How are you feeling now? I dare say I broke through your fever just in time." Her voice was as calm and soothing as ever.

Propping himself up on one elbow with the help of Cassandra, Evan found all his friends huddled about a campfire. Dijin was nowhere to be found. "What is happening?" Evan was flustered. "What is going on? Where are we?"

"Peace, Evan," Cassandra soothed with a tight smile. *If only he knew how dangerous our situation really is. But he has just been through so much . . .*

"We have cleared Stanbury and now stand on the edge of Marden, the land of pools," Helios spoke up.

"I was so worried about moving you," Dawn chimed in, "but Cassandra here promised that you would be alright. It is so fortunate that she came across us."

Fortunate indeed, Evan thought. *She has been keeping an eye on us. And for that, I am very grateful.* He clasped the priestess's hand tightly. The look in her eyes showed that she understood the situation. They loved each other, but could not afford to do anything about it. That was how plain and simple it was. Neither one would deviate from their path of duty, for they knew full well the desperate state that Fadreama was in.

"What of Sienna and her family?" asked Evan. "I am afraid my mind is a bit foggy." He tried desperately to shake Dijin away. Darius was oddly silent.

Alan stepped forward with a surprisingly pained look in his eyes. "The fire . . . it was burning out of control." He paused. "The flames were so intense and so very . . . angry." Alan ran a hand through his hair. "Sienna was determined to find her family, a family that by all reasonable logic was already long dead. I say it bluntly only because that is just the way it is."

Dawn placed a hand softly on Alan's shoulder as he continued, "She raced this way and that way. Evan, I could scarcely keep up with her! It was so difficult to notice human scents through the flames, but at last I caught it . . . strongly. It was blood . . . spilled human blood." He closed his eyes against the memory. "Sienna's family had been tortured and killed in the main dungeon. Ralston just shut up the room and left the bodies there. Sienna . . . I had taken her to be a fighter, a level-headed lady. I mean, she knew so much about survival, but I guess everyone has their breaking point. We can only take so much. Eventually, something inside of us snaps and we are broken."

Evan hesitated and then spoke in a dry voice, "She is dead, then."

"There was nothing I could do," Alan replied quietly. "There was only one option left for me and that was to leave." He looked back at Dawn. "My obligations lay beyond the princess of Stanbury and her unfortunate family. Call me callous if you will, Helios, but I speak my truth loud and clear."

"I never said anything," Helios responded in an even tone. He had been very quiet since Dawn's outburst earlier. His heart ached more painfully than he could ever express. *Did I send Alan into a dangerous situation deliberately? Even I am not sure if I did or not . . .*

"And now, Cassandra, what will you do?" asked Evan, staring deeply into her soft eyes.

"I think you know the answer to that question very well, your highness," she replied, addressing him formally. Her heart pounded in her chest, but her face never betrayed a beat.

"Come with us. Stay with us." Evan held Cassandra's hand firmly. Never before in his life had he desired something so much. Evan felt a strange tremor in the Web of Life. Something was coming loose—perhaps the very fabric of the world. *At the end of all things I want you by my side, Cassandra.*

She seemed to read his thoughts, for she replied, "In the end, I will be with you. But until that time, I have too much to do. Madame has charged me with clearing the evil spirits out of the land and helping those souls who are trapped to cross over. I cannot abandon them—not when the end is so close. It was Madame's last wish." Her voice was strained as she said this.

Evan nodded. He had expected nothing less of Cassandra. "Then I shall do my part as well. And when the time comes, as we know it will, I will be waiting for you. *Evan* shall be waiting for you, *Cassandra.*" It was obvious that Evan had no intention of allowing Darius to overtake his body for the sake of Kiara. *Yes you love her, Darius, but you had your time. Now give me what is left of mine.*

With that, Cassandra nodded and straightened up. She turned to face the others who had been watching the exchange in respectful, if not awkward, silence. "I expect you understand what must be done now. You have but one mission and must abandon all others."

"The Crystal Points," Mizu suddenly spoke up. She had been oddly quiet and pensive since Evan's absorption of the Fire element.

"Yes," Cassandra confirmed with a resolute nod. "You must visit each one and absorb your respective element. Each of you have been chosen to protect and represent one of the elements. It is no longer safe for them to live openly in Fadreama. The environment here has become too unstable and unbalanced, thanks to the dealings of Ralston Radburn and Magica. Once you absorb your element into your body, you will hold it until at last it is time for the purification to occur. That will come, I think, when the fourth element has been absorbed. Then Spirit will cleanse Fadreama and . . . I know not what then." She almost faltered and looked slightly afraid. "All the Fragments of Cardew will be purified . . . that much I can guess. You must be careful though, for the closer you get to a Crystal Point the more corruption you may face. Remember, if Ralston has taken over, the Fragments will be attracted to the Crystal Point."

"Water," Mizu whispered. "We are nearest to the Pool of Water in Marden. My element . . . She is calling out to me. I can hear her voice screaming in agony . . . It is Nimue, the Lady of the Pools."

Ian touched Mizu's arm lightly. "Mizu . . ." he whispered, feeling a terrible fear well up inside of him. *The Sisters told me I had to live to record the truth, but if Mizu needed me, I would be there for her in a heartbeat, danger or no. And surely, we both would die . . .*

Mizu shrugged Ian's hand away. "Don't, Ian," she said firmly. "We both know what we have to do. We both know how this all will end . . ." *In heartbreak for all . . .* she thought bitterly.

"You are right, Mizu," Cassandra nodded. "The nearest Crystal Point is located just north of here in, Marden, the Land of Pools. It is a strange land, or so I have been told, ethereal but with pleasant weather. The entire land is said to be covered in widely spaced birch trees with a multitude of clear pools dappled about. I have never been there, but I have heard it is beautiful, if not, hypnotic. You must be on your guard, for I fear Ralston is already on his way to the sacred Pool."

"Likely planning to poison it, just as he did Fire," Dawn mused with folded arms. "He cannot control it on his own. He said as much to me. He needs help and," she turned to Mizu, "I think you are now in danger."

Despite Mizu's protests, Ian again took her arm. "But do not fear. We will stand by you and protect you. The element of Water will be absorbed and you will be safe, I promise."

"I am not afraid," Mizu replied quietly. "I know what I must do and afterwards, I know where I will end up. For I am immortal and all of this is just one moment in eternity. I envy you all, for no matter what terrible things await us, you will always have death. I, however, do not have such a luxury. Not even the luxury to be born anew and forget."

Now Cassandra brushed off her skirts and stared up at the moon briefly. "Enough with this moping!" she declared firmly. "Ralson has a tremendous lead over us." From her satchel she withdrew several Crystal Roses. "Courtesy of dear Madame Iris," she said and nearly choked over the name. *Dear Madame, what will become of you, trapped under Magica's dark dome in Devona? How I wish you were here to advise me in these evil times.* "Take these Roses and get to Merlin, quickly," Cassandra instructed, referring to the capital city of Marden, "for it is there that the sacred Pool of Water lies."

At last Evan got to his feet and wobbled a little unsteadily. "Cassandra—" She cut him off.

"No, Evan. I will head north on my own. I have things to do, just as you do. But our paths will cross again, trust me. I am never really so very far away." For a moment the couple just stared at each other, as though drinking in the image of one another. They did not touch, however, and at last, Cassandra turned in a flurry of priestess robes and wandered out into the darkness.

Why, Cassandra, thought Evan, *do you take on everything alone? Surely it is not your fate to be so solitary? Part of me, as divided as I already am, goes with you. That part, is my heart.* Cassandra had not looked back.

CHAPTER 9

Call of the Waves

"**W**HO AM I? WELL I'm surprised that you don't know! My name is practically *sacred* in the southern countries! Well, I suppose you are very isolated up here in the north. My name is Queen Alice of Algernon," Magica announced in smooth voice, though there was something forced beneath it. She stood before the king and queen of Marden in their ethereal seaside palace.

There was something different about the tall, lithe and willowy people in Marden. When they walked, they seemed to float. When they spoke, it was like music to the listener. It was such a contrast to the burly strong folk in Stanbury. In truth, the people of Marden seemed very much like the Acjah—elves—Dawn had met in the shining garden of Etain. In some stories, it was even claimed that the people of Marden, were elves who had chosen to live mortal lives. There were various other tales each claiming the same thing—that the people of Etain were descended from immortals. Naturally time had erased all truth in the matter, leaving only tantalizing hints and clues.

"Queen Alice of Algernon?" Queen L'eau raised a silver eyebrow in disbelief. "I am well versed in the accomplishments of Queen Alice. I admire her very much, though I have never had the privilege of meeting her directly." She smoothed her flowing blue gown which had a gauzy sheen, similar to sea foam. Her voice revealed an elegant accent and her hair shimmered like sunlight on water.

"Then I am sure you will not hesitate in showing me your kingdom's Crystal Point, The Pool of Water," Magica continued in a voice that only appeared calm at the surface. A keen observer, such as the King and Queen, could see the tension.

Bent over on one knee some distance behind Magica, posing as a servant, Lance gritted his teeth. *Wretch that Magica is! Even as a slave she is trying to thwart me! Anyone with eyes can see there is something odd about her behaviour! How am I to trick the royals into helping me if I cannot gain their trust? That Creature is not as strong as I thought, if he cannot force Magica to speak his words!*

"You are trembling," King Bleu observed, eyeing her carefully. He was dressed in a tunic of royal blue, sewn with silver threads. His beard was white and long, though he did not seem aged, for his face held no wrinkles, his eyes glistened keenly and his hands were smooth and clear. "We had always been led to believe that Queen Alice is a strong and dignified woman. You seem beaten down and conflicted."

"What are you suggesting, exactly?" Magica felt herself exclaim. She was only in her original form because Ralston had desired it as a way to trick the royal family. As much as she looked and sounded like her old self, this was not truly Magica, for she was being controlled by her Creature, who in turn was answering to Ralston. Magica could see and feel herself, though she had no control of her own. *Soon,* she thought bitterly, *my mind will spiral back into the nothingness. I will have no thoughts, no voice. I will not exist. This is my only chance to cry out! But there is no one to help me. No one is listening. Alice cannot help me and I do not think I can depend upon her daughter. My poor Kane . . . The best I can do is try to impede Ralston in any way I can!*

Magica screamed inside the Creature's head—the Creature she had created using pieces of Ralston himself. She continued to scream until suddenly the scream erupted from her own lips and echoed off the royal chamber walls.

King Bleu and Queen L'eau stared at her in surprise. "You are *not* the good Queen Alice of Algernon," Queen L'eau pointed out sternly. "Who are you?"

Using all the strength she had, Magica spoke quickly, knowing that she had precious little time to speak. "No, I am not Queen Alice, only her poor wretched cousin!"

The King and Queen gasped at this revelation and turned to their guards.

Magica continued, "Truth be told, my life has been nothing but sorrow and it is all because of . . . because of . . ." *Not because of Alice* she thought. Magica fought to keep control of her mind, for she could feel the Creature taking over again. *No!* "Ralston!" She finally screamed. "He ruined my life, murdered my parents and made me into this angry, vengeful, bitter-hearted woman! I hate Denzel! I rue the day my parents fled there!" she cried and then narrowed her eyes and clenched her fists. "But most of all," she turned to face the angry figure of Lord Lance de Felda—Ralston—now standing behind her, "I hate, I hate, I hate RALSTON RADBURN!"

As these words left her lips, Magica could feel hot tears rolling down her cheeks. "Everything I have ever done, ever devoted myself to, has been out of hatred," she whispered. She turned back to face the shocked royal couple. "He took away my innocence and the only one who could have possibly defeated him is dying. I have been a pawn all my life. Even when I thought I was working in my own interests, I wasn't. It was always according to *his* plan. So much has been lost, so much wasted. What I have done cannot be undone, but I *refuse* to be a pawn. I would rather not exist at all! Do your own dirty work from now on Ralston!" Magica turned her eyes, which at this moment had clarity in them, towards King Bleu and Queen L'eau. "I would tell you to run, but it is already too late." Two large tears rolled down her cheeks. "I am sorry, for everything! For everything, I am so sorry. The only one who could remember me in a state of innocence is already dead, so my memory will persist as a lie. Thus, I am punished and we are even, Alice."

Queen L'eau made a move to rush forward towards Magica, but an enormous commotion at the back of the room stopped her. There stood Lance, glowing red with anger. Behind him stood Kage, Itami and Kedamono—the Shadow Senshi. Lance clenched his fist, gripping a large Fragment of Cardew. Magica disappeared and in her place stood the Creature she had made. Ralston spat on the ground in his rage and declared, "Kill them all."

* * *

Mizu was standing on the beach of a small island in the White Sands Bay. As she stared out across the glittering crystal clear ocean, the sand sparkled like diamonds. She sighed, feeling the impending crisis weigh heavily upon her shoulders. *I am next,* she thought.

Using the Crystal Roses from Cassandra, the group had basically island hopped their way along the coastline. It was a mentally draining experience to rapidly use Rose after Rose, for it required so much coordinated concentration. Now, they had stopped for a rest, just one transportation away from the capital city of Merlin, which was where the next Crystal Point lay.

"We should not simply rush into battle weak and exhausted," Helios advised while stretching his neck which was sore from the strain. "Likely something highly unpleasant awaits us in Merlin. Such a thing will keep until morning."

And so the group had opted to rest for the night on the island the local villagers called 'Kanakike'. It was a very tropical sort of island for being so far north. In fact, winter seemed to have all but disappeared in this beach land with its glittering sand and palm trees. Delicate waterfalls cascaded from small cliffs located near the center of the island, creating misty rainbows which constantly danced and changed.

"A bit like Alexandria," Evan had commented, mostly to himself, refusing to admit he was capable of feeling homesick. *I think I shall never again see that world or my Mother . . .*

Dawn replied quickly, "I thought it more like the elfin land, myself."

"In any case, it is truly beautiful," Ian smiled, breathing in the dewy evening air. "It's hard to believe what carnage lies ahead on the mainland."

At that moment, a figure appeared in the distance, soon followed by others. "Villagers," Alan sighed. "As if we needed the company."

"Shush," Dawn whispered. "They may be able to provide nicer accommodations for the evening. I think we could all use a good rest."

The villagers did not appear to be hostile. They were rather roundish and short, dressed in skirts made of dry grass with seashells strategically placed on their torsos. All the villagers had jet black hair and the loveliest almond eyes which shone with their warm smiles of greeting. The young ladies, who were not quite so round, laughed and offered gifts of sweetly scented flowers.

"This is a paradise!" Ian declared with a smile. Gently he picked up his lute and began to strum out a hauntingly romantic tune. Instantly the island girls had surrounded him in adoration. Ian beamed and soaked in the attention. Mizu simply rolled her eyes and stared out blankly towards the sea.

Meanwhile, one particularly large man who appeared to be the chief came forward. "Greetings," he spoke with an accent, indicating that this was not his first language.

"Our apologies for intruding upon your island like this," Dawn offered, stepping out to meet him. "I am—" She was cut off by the chief.

"It no matter who you are or where you from," he said with slightly faltering grammar. "What matter is, where you are going!" His small dark eyes twinkled with knowledge. "I am Chief Ailani. These my people." He indicated to those around him, as well as a speck of a village in the distance. "For all time in Kanakike, we have legend. It tell of strange group appearing from air. We wait long time to see this."

"It means something important to your people, Chief Ailani?" asked Dawn, doing her best to pronounce his name.

The Chief gave a sort of half smile and looked sad for a moment. "It mean 'the end'."

*   *   *

It was very late in the night when Mizu crept softly out of her bed of sweetly scented woven grasses. She could not sleep, for the anxiety of what lay ahead had knotted her stomach. *It is not the Crystal Point which frightens me so,* she thought. *Rather, it is what will happen after, when all is said and done. When Dawn does what she is destined to do . . . I am afraid of what will become of me, for I shall outlast all of this. All of the events which are happening . . . Everything and everyone is just a drop in the ocean of time.*

Mizu made her way across the cool white sands and stood on the shore of the ocean. The moon was a waxing crescent, growing brighter each night, as though urging Fadreama on towards a great purification.

Mizu sat down upon the powdery soft sands and grasped a handful. As she gently let the grains fall between her fingers, a voice behind her said, "We do not often experience so peaceful a night."

"Ian," Mizu breathed and turned her head. She could feel her heart speed up just a little and she immediately clenched her fists.

Ian came closer and sat down beside her without hesitation. Turning his face up at the moonlight he said, "I am sorry about earlier . . . with the island girls, I mean. I know that hurt you, even if you won't admit it." Mizu did not reply to this, but simply shrugged her shoulders. "I can't help but revel in the attention," Ian admitted ruefully. "That's just me, I guess. Of course, it really is no excuse."

"I have already told you, I am used to your quirks," Mizu finally found her voice again. She had been too astonished by his abrupt apology to reply earlier. The moonlight now shone through her hair, making the soft sea green streaks glitter and glow like the rippling ocean before them.

And before either of them knew it, Ian leaned in towards Mizu's face and kissed her gently on the lips. It was a soft and warm kiss, the kind that showed a feeling more pure and full than anything wild or passionate could convey. This kiss expressed everything that even Ian, for all his creative talents, could not put into words. And Mizu . . . Mizu returned the kiss, in spite of herself. She melted into it and for the first time in her human form, she felt complete.

"I can't believe this," Dawn whispered to Evan and Alan, who were hovering behind her as they watched Mizu and Ian from the door of their hut.

"I say, it's about darn time," Evan nodded approvingly. "Maybe now Ian will focus on the mission, rather than on impressing every girl we meet."

At this, Alan laughed. "You can't possibly think one kiss will change his personality, Evan! Honestly!"

"*Honestly* will you all come back here and get some rest," urged Helios sulkily from back within the hut. He refused to demean himself by watching their friends on the beach.

Mizu and Ian had now parted and quickly the Glintel turned her face away to hide the blush. "Ian, I do not know what will happen in the future."

"No one does," Ian smiled ruefully. "All we have is each moment. That's why we need to make the most of them—it may be all we have."

Mizu nodded. "You are right, Ian. I will try not to think of what is to come, but rather what is at hand. Though it . . ." She trailed off. "Do you . . . do you hear that voice?"

Ian shook his head. "I hear nothing except the waves and your breathing."

Suddenly Mizu jumped to her feet. "It is Nalopa! I can hear her calling out to me!"

"Mizu . . ." Ian stood up and touched her arm. "I really think we need some rest."

At that moment, a giant blue orb appeared to hover over the water. Inside was a beautiful woman with robes like the waves. "Mizu," she said in an other worldly voice. "It is I, Naolpa. I am calling you home. Come with me now."

Mizu's eyes seemed to glass over and her face held very little expression. "Nalopa . . ." she whispered stepping forward.

Ian narrowed his eyes and firmly grabbed her arm. "No, Mizu! That is not Nalopa! Nalopa wants you to fulfill your mission on land! It doesn't make sense for her to be calling you back so suddenly!"

But Mizu was entranced by the floating woman and easily broke free of Ian's grip. She strode forward, across the water, hovering above it.

"Everyone!" Ian screamed. "Get out here!"

It was too late. Mizu and the woman were gone.

CHAPTER 10

Stolen Memories

"**I**AN, YOU HAVE TO calm down or you will be of no assistance to Mizu," Evan told his friend firmly. Ian was pacing about frantically in front of their small island hut.

"How can I possibly calm down, Evan?" Ian retorted passionately. "That image had to have been Magica! Only she could concoct such a thing! And of course it is Ralston holding her leash! That monster wants Mizu so he can gain control of the next Crystal Point!" His eyes blazed with emotion that was strong, even for him. The very winds seemed to whip up with his anger and there were waves out upon the ocean.

"Well obviously that is why Mizu has been taken," Helios soothed. "We all know that. But we cannot make our next move rashly or we may be endangering *everything.*"

"By everything, you just mean Dawn," Ian snapped back and then his face fell. "I am sorry, Dawn, but this whole world is starting to bring me to the point of madness."

"No, cousin," Dawn smiled sadly, "love has done that to you." Though she spoke with a quiet calm, inside she was quaking. *My dearest friend, Mizu! How dare Ralston seek to use you like this! Please hold on and wait for us! We will rescue you and show Ralston that we are not to be underestimated!* "Helios," she said in a voice that demanded obedience, "bring out the Crystal Roses. We are heading to the mainland."

*   *   *

Mizu's eyes fluttered open and when her focus returned, she found herself in a great cavern with walls that sparkled and glittered with various shades of blue gemstones. She was sitting, slumped over, on a throne of crystal, tinged with a faint shade of blue. Veins and variation inside the crystal throne sparkled from the multitude of candles which surrounded Mizu. In the center of the room, lay a great circular pool of water. Its surface was completely calm and reflected the gemstone ceiling like a mirror. If Mizu had known, she might have mistaken it for a Virtue Temple.

As Mizu became more conscious of herself, she realized that she was dressed in a foreign gown of blue, with several gauzy layers. Sapphire gems adorned her wrists, neck and ears. She shook her head and placed one hand over her eyes, trying to focus on what had happened. However, try as she might, Mizu could not remember who she was, where she was from, or what she was doing in this strange cavern. Something at the back of her mind was screaming for attention, but she could not bring herself to acknowledge it. *What is wrong with me? I don't know anything . . .* Panic began to bubble inside her, until a voice next to her spoke, "My Queen, what is wrong?"

"Q . . . queen?" Mizu stuttered and looked at the crystal throne next to her. There sat a man of extraordinary handsomeness. His face seemed to radiate energy and she was immediately calmed by his presence.

"My dearest, you must have nodded off," the man smiled gently and touched her hand. His hair was shoulder length and a glossy hue of deep brown. Mizu felt it was gorgeous. The man's eyes were such an endearing shade of hazel that suited his tan complexion perfectly. He was, in a sense, the perfectly proportioned man, dressed fashionably in a deep navy tunic with silver trim.

"Oh . . . yes . . . I must have," Mizu agreed, but somehow felt that wasn't true.

"Do you know who you are? Do you know where you are? Do you even know me?" the handsome man fired off each question without waiting for a response. He then took Mizu gently by the shoulders and stared deeply into her eyes. "You are Queen L'eau of Marden and I am your husband, King Bleu. We are currently within the Crystal Point of the Water Element. This is the sacred Pool of Water."

"Of course," Mizu mused. Her thoughts were swimming about rapidly in her head, reassembling and trying to make sense of her situation. *I don't remember, but his words have truth in them. Somehow I cannot doubt him. I believe everything he says.*

"And now," continued King Bleu, "do you remember why we came to the sacred Pool in the first place? Do you remember? It was, after all, your idea."

"I . . . I'm sorry, but I don't recall," Mizu admitted, finding it strange that her husband did not question her lack of memories.

King Bleu took Mizu in his arms and held her closely as he brought her to her feet. "It's okay, my love. I will refresh your mind. Just listen to the sound of my voice. Block everything but my words." Mizu nodded weakly. "Excellent. We came here because you were worried about the safety of the Water Element. You feared it was no longer prudent to allow it to remain unprotected. And so, you decided to put the element under the protection of the strongest person you could find, our dear and trusted friend, Lord Lance de Felda." At these words, Lance entered the chamber with a bow and flourish.

"At your service, Your Graces," he said with a honey-coated voice. "My life is but to serve the two of you."

Upon hearing his voice, Mizu felt uneasy. *Why does this man, who seems respectable enough, send a chill to my very soul? I feel that I should hate him and yet I can think of no logical reason why.*

"But Your Graces, we can waste no time in transferring the Water Element to me," Lance urged. "There is danger approaching, so we must not delay!"

"Come, my sweet," King Bleu said as he led Mizu along by the hand.

"I don't know how," Mizu stammered as they approached the mirror-like pool. She stared, wide-eyed into its depths and for a moment, images flashed before her eyes. She saw faces, places and events that seemed beyond her reach. In particular, one young man's face intrigued her. He had unruly blond hair and intense blue eyes. She could not help but wonder where she had known him or if indeed she ever had.

Lord Lance de Felda's voice broke her thoughts. "Your Grace? Do you see something in the water? If so, I suggest you ignore it. The Pool is known to play tricks with the eyes and mind. Mizu somehow felt afraid to say that it was not her eyes and mind that were confused, but rather, her heart.

"I am sorry, my lord," she replied quickly, as King Bleu squeezed her arm again softly.

"It is okay, my darling, but please, time is of the essence. You must transfer the element of Water over to Lord Lance, so that he might protect it from harm," King Bleu instructed.

"But I honestly do not know what to do," Mizu pleaded. "I have no idea how to call forth the Water element, much less its spirit."

Wretched woman! Lance thought in frustration. *Her friends are quickly approaching! We haven't time to waste!* He glared at Magica's Creature, urging him to find a way.

*   *   *

"That should have been the royal palace!" Evan exclaimed, pointing to a smoldering and burned out structure.

"It seems we are too late for the royal family," Dawn whispered sadly. "So much destruction." *Does this world even deserve to exist? No! I mustn't think like that. So long as just one heart remains pure, then this world is justified.*

"I smell blood," Alan observed. "And it is not that of the dead, but rather, of one who is on the verge."

"Can you locate it?" Dawn asked, fearful that it might be Mizu. *No, it could not be her. She is far too valuable to Ralston.*

With a quick nod, Alan was dashing off towards the rubble. Evan, meanwhile, felt his heart pounding. "The Web of Life is shattered here," he sighed. "This land will never be the same. So much loss and destruction . . . I cannot describe what it feels like."

"It does not take your abilities to know of the destruction here," Helios responded quietly. "One need only look around at the toppled trees, torn up earth and polluted pools."

Suddenly Alan called out, "I've found someone! I think it's the Queen!" The others raced towards the destroyed palace and, sure enough, it was Queen L'eau, fatally injured, but still clinging to life. Her gown was blood soaked near her heart and her face was a ghastly shade.

"You have come for me, Alice," the dying Queen whispered. "I knew that you would."

Taken aback, Dawn quickly regained herself and replied, "Yes, I am here now. Everything is going to be okay. Please, what happened?"

Queen L'eau licked her lips and whispered hoarsely, "Ralston Radburn."

"Naturally," Evan gritted his teeth.

"Where is Mizu? Have you seen a beautiful Glintel woman?" Ian blurted out.

For a moment, Queen L'eau managed a spark of life. "Take me to the Crystal Point, The Pool of Water. I wish to die there and it is there that you shall find Ralston." She grunted under the exertion of speaking.

"Brace yourself, everyone," whispered Evan. "The Web of Life is shaking."

"Old friends," Helios muttered turning around.

There stood the Shadow Senshi, complete with Gamren and a host of walking dead.

"Get out of my way!" screamed Ian in a fury. "I must find Mizu!"

CHAPTER 11

Lady of the Pool

"SIMPLY CALL OUT TO the Water," suggested Lance. "Or perhaps dip your hands into the pool itself. Maybe the simple act of touch will activate the transfer."

"I suppose there is no harm in trying," Mizu admitted slowly. "As long as you are certain I have the ability to actually do this. I can't imagine how you know."

Lance's eyes narrowed, "Oh, I know."

Graceful, as only a Glintel could be, Mizu kneeled next to the reflective pool and slid her hands softly into the warm water. At once it felt as though her hands were bathed in glowing energy. It was so very inviting that she felt she wanted more and more of her body immersed within the liquid. Deeper she moved her arms until the water was up to her forearms, then elbows and shoulders.

"I think that is deep enough, darling," King Bleu said, slightly uneasily. He shot Lance an uncertain look.

"No, no," Lance replied, "let her do this in her own way." *With her mind under my control, we should be in no danger from the Water Element, as we were with Fire.*

The Water seemed to be calling out to Mizu, inviting her to come all the way in. Mizu's face was a mere breath away from the surface. The water rippled gently when she exhaled. *It's so warm and soothing,* she thought. *It couldn't hurt for me to enter, I think . . .* Without another thought, Mizu gently slipped her head and body into the water, diving down deep to the center of the pool.

"I can hardly see her," King Bleu, who was in fact Magica's Creature, observed. He squinted his eyes to make out Mizu's blurry shape. "The water is too reflective."

"Just let her be for a minute," Lance said tightly. "This may be how she absorbs the element. Then, she will give it directly to me."

Mizu was hovering in the center of the pool and finding, to her immense surprise, that she could breathe! As she gently moved her arms and legs to keep upright, a willowy figure appeared before her. The woman had long, flowing hair that shimmered like sunlight on a trickling stream. She was a shapely woman, representing the exact ideal of what a healthy woman in her prime should look like. It was easy to judge, for the woman was clad in nothing at all. She was the supreme feminine and her face expressed all the emotions in the world. It was as though she could feel the pain and sorrow, but also all the joy and hope at once. A glowing blue crystal hung in the center of her forehead on a silver thread. The woman reached out and placed a hand upon Mizu's cheek. She stroked Mizu's face softly and said, "You must know me, for I have always been surrounding you, all your life. You are so special, Mizu. You and I are twinned. I have chosen you to hold my energy until the end. I am the Water. I am Nimue, Lady of the Pools."

Mizu nodded slowly. "Yes, I think I know you, but my mind is cloudy."

"You are being controlled and poisoned," Nimue explained. "You are not a queen. You are Mizu, an immortal Glintel in human guise. You became human to help a friend." Nimue held Mizu's head with both her hands and touched her forehead to Mizu's. "Hear me and know my words are true. Remember who you are. Know who you will become. Accept it."

Mizu closed her eyes and felt a powerful warmth seeping into her slender limbs. The elegance of grace of Nimue, The Water, was passing into her. With Nimue's cleansing strength, Mizu felt the poison of Ralston being washed from her mind. Her body felt dirty from The Creature's touch and her mind felt violated to the highest degree. Now, Nimue's outrage at the state of Fadreama, merged with Mizu's. Her false clothing melted away and for the first time, she felt empowered to be a human woman. *These female bodies hold more strength than they belie.*

The water within the pool had begun to bubble, as if boiling. Steam rose in wispy tendrils from the surface. "What is happening?" asked Magica's Creature, raising a shapely eyebrow at the surface of the water.

"Stay back," Ralston warned. "She is absorbing the Water Element. It may be an explosive force. We must wait for the transfer to be complete. Then, she will submit herself to me." He smiled eerily and clasped his hands.

The Creature, who was made of Ralston himself, nodded in agreement. It was difficult to say whether or not the Creature had a soul and separate consciousness. Was he an individual or merely an extension of Ralston? Even Ralston himself could not tell for certain, though the Creature obeyed readily enough. At the very least, Ralston was rid of Magica once and for all and if that was the only thing the Creature did for him, he would be satisfied.

Mizu was twirling and swirling, limbs gliding gracefully through the water. She was filled with the element and sensed the danger lurking just above her on the surface. Her eyes frosted over, as Nimue took hold. In a gigantic burst of energy, Mizu rode a powerful jet of water up to the surface and hovered above Ralston and the Creature.

"How dare you!" she screamed at Ralston, whose expression was one of defiance.

"You are mine! I own you!" he spat back with arrogant confidence. "The spell on your mind is not so easily dissipated as that!"

Mizu clutched the back of her head, feeling her mind being pulled in two directions. Ralston pulled back and Nimue pulled forward. The result was excruciating pain.

"Now," smiled Ralston, "give me your power."

*   *   *

Evan struck up a barrier just in time to save them all from a deadly slash by Kage's razor sharp scythe. Kage flew back from the impact and landed some distance away.

"It's been awhile, eh fairy boy?" asked Kage with a devious grin. "I've been waiting to finish you off, once and for all!"

Evan was down on one knee from the strain of having used the barrier. He leaned heavily on his sword, as a droplet of sweat rolled down his temple. "You really are dense, Kage. Surely you know by now that you're no match for me!" He got to his feet, feeling the strength of Fire burning within his soul.

Kage made a sour face and screamed to the other Senshi and Gamren, "Kill them now!"

Dawn turned to Alan quickly, "What will we do about Queen L'eau?"

"She is fatally wounded . . ." Alan replied uneasily. "We have to defend ourselves right now."

Evan let loose a battle cry as he sliced through the synergy of several of Gamren's walking dead. Helios whisked out his gigantic arrows taking down some of Gamren's minions. "This may be a battle we cannot win," he whispered under his breath.

"Leave the Queen with me," Ian said, indicating towards a slight hollow by a group of tall trees. "I will take care of her there, while you take care of them. After all, I have no weapons, only a lute and some writing tablets."

Alan and Dawn nodded. "Be safe, Ian."

Now the two turned to face the battle that was already underway. Kedamono was knocking down trees left and right, sending deafening cracking sounds through the air. "Those trees belong to the Acjah!" Dawn cried, drawing forth her magical bow. "Light of the Earth! Combine with my bow and lend it your strength!" Just as before, there was a brief flash of light, as the elfin weapon fused with her bow. Dawn aimed a green arrow. "Let the trees fight back!" She released the arrow which struck Kedamono in the shin, doing little more than annoy him. However the magic spread out from the arrow, awakening the trees left standing. Their roots and limbs creaked with life, as they stretched towards the brute. The trees were now attacking Kedamono's limbs, just as he had attacked theirs.

"See how it feels!" Dawn cried in triumph, only to have Alan sweep her into his arms and leap into the air. Itami's halberd was stuck in the ground where she had just been standing. Astonished, Dawn looked at Alan and whispered, "Thank you."

"Don't thank me yet," Alan warned. "We're not in the clear." He alighted on the ground and placed Dawn back on her feet as Itami rushed towards them from one side, while the walking dead of Gamren approached from the other. Alan pulled out his bow and charged it with dark energy. Dawn could feel the cold emanating from it. She shivered, but there was no time to reprimand him, as the ghosts were advancing quickly.

Suddenly an image flashed before Dawn's eyes. It was of Mizu—she was screaming and in pain. Dawn clutched her head. *Ralston!* She thought quickly. *We have to get to the Pool of Water soon! Hold on Mizu!* Dawn's mind then went back to the words of Artemis, one of the Three Sisters. Artemis's words rang clear through Dawn's head, *'Magic has its time and place, but you need to be able to do more than defend yourself—you need to know how to fight and you don't have to be a man to do this.'* Dawn's grip on her bow tightened. She nodded her head with decision. *Mizu is in trouble and I am going to get her back my way!*

"You take on Itami!" Dawn told Alan over her shoulder. "Leave Gamren and his cohorts to me." Before Alan could reply, Dawn was racing into the fray. Hitching her bow to her back, Dawn withdrew the elegant sword left to her by the Three Sisters. It did not contain magic, but it contained Dawn's own energy and will. Holding the sword high, she crashed into the army of dead, slashing and maneuvering her way through them. Dawn's advantage was her size—she was small and therefore could pick her way around the crushing blows of the ghosts. The ghosts were not really injured, so to speak, but they *were* taking damage. And Dawn was truly in a frenzy. She blocked from her mind all thoughts that the corpses had once been people with families, jobs and homes. Her desire to save Mizu was driving her and she was hardly aware of her success. Onward she plowed through the ghosts until she sensed a different sort of energy—a living one. Dawn's senses returned as she focused on the energy. *It's Gamren himself,* she thought. *He's nearby! If only I could get at him! For all he has done to Mizu, I must purify him! The Fragment of Cardew he contains is the source of his power! I must remove it from him! If I can do that he will die, but be at peace at least. Sally is waiting for him I think and Ralston will no longer be able to use him!*

Ducking down to avoid the swinging arm of a corpse, Dawn fished the Stone of Desire from her belt pouch which she had slung around her beautiful dress from Stanbury. A quick thought of Gamren was all it took to send the stone into a brilliant pulsating light. *He's here!* Dawn followed the light in one hand, while wielding her sword in the other. It was an amazing sight—one that none could have expected. Here was Princess Dawn, fighting her way through a legion of the dead, alone yet! It was not so very long ago that she was a child who knew nothing of the world beyond Dalton Castle. How things had changed!

And all at once, Dawn saw him. Gamren was standing by a clear pool of water, watching over his minions. For Dawn, it was as though time had stopped. She saw the old man and she saw what the Fragment of Cardew had done to his sorrow over losing his young wife. The system in Devona had failed him and he had been treated unjustly. The Fragment had latched onto his pain and multiplied it until it was out of control. Dawn knew in her heart that this man had no time left to spend upon the earth. She had to free him.

Gamren was too shocked for words when he saw Dawn coming at him through the army of dead. *It's that girl and she's is glowing white! So bright, it hurts my eyes!*

To Gamren, it was as though the sun were moving towards him at the break of dawn. He shielded his eyes with his hands, but the light seemed to shine right through them. Dawn's energy was lighting up the woods and reflected in a sparkling array of diamonds off the pools.

"Your time on this earth has come to an end, Gamren," Dawn said in a calm voice. She had sheathed her sword and replaced the Stone of Desire in her pouch pocket. "I feel your pain and sorrow, so I have come to set you free," she explained. Her eyes held only compassion and determination. "All this fighting . . . it is not for you, old man. Let go of this all and join your wife on the other side. Let these corpses return to dust and let any lost souls you stole see the light. Sally is calling out to you. She misses you greatly and hates to see you like this. It pains her to see what you have become . . . how you have been misused."

"The light, so bright, so warm . . ." Gamren fell to his knees in desperate sadness. His body began to heave with sobs. He could speak no words, for he was in awe of what he saw before him: a young lady in a white, flowing dress that seemed woven of light. Every strand of her hair was filled with light and warmth. Where her feet touched the grass, little white flowers sprung up. *The Goddess . . .* he thought in his foggy mind.

Dawn now approached Gamren and lay her hands on his trembling shoulders. "It is time to let go. Let the light wash you clean." Indeed the light was glowing brightly now and all the others around could not help but turn to look.

"What the . . ." murmured Kage, as he paused in his confrontation with Evan.

"Dawn," was all Alan, Evan and Helios could say. As for Ian, he was madly scribbling on a tablet.

When the light gradually faded away, Gamren lay dead in a circle of tiny white flowers and every walking corpse was gone—every soul, crossed over.

CHAPTER 12

Mizu's Destiny

*A*GREAT BURST OF PURE light energy shook the lands of Marden, causing a few gleaming crystals to fall from the roof of the sacred cave where Nimue and Ralston were doing battle over Mizu's mind. Ralston looked up at the falling stones and frowned. *What is going on out there? Can't I depend on those Shadow Senshi to do anything right?*

* * *

The Shadow Senshi were fleeing. The fate of Gamren had been so sudden and unexpected that they had not known what to make of it. Rather than stick around and find out if such a fate could be theirs, Kage had ordered a hasty retreat, knowing full well that Ralston would be angry. However, circumstances being what they currently were, Kage didn't much care what Ralston thought. *Let him deal with this mess,* he thought bitterly.

"Dawn!" Alan raced towards the princess who no longer was glowing. She turned around solemnly and held out her hand. A shining Fragment lay there. Helios and Evan approached Dawn as well—Evan in awe and Helios concealed as ever. "I am truly amazed, cousin," said Evan.

"No time!" yelled Ian from the hollow where he hid. "The Queen is fading fast and Mizu may be as well! The Queen keeps whispering that we must help her!"

"The Pool is calling," Dawn whispered, clenching her fists.

* * *

Why is this happening to me? Mizu thought to herself, as the battle for her mind continued. She could hardly recall who she was or why she was in this agonizing situation.

"Queen L'eau!" Lance roared in his commanding and handsome voice. "Give the element to me! Give me the Water! You must listen, for the safety of all! What sort of queen would put all she cares about in danger? What sort of queen are you?"

"She . . . is not one at all . . ." whispered a faint voice from the cave entrance.

Alan stood menacingly in the mouth of the cave, holding a barely conscious Queen L'eau in his arms.

At this appearance, Lance belted out a string of unmentionable curses. Helios stepped around Alan and drew his bow, aiming it squarely at Lance. "Let the Glintel go, or you will feel my wrath."

"And mine!" shouted Ian from behind Helios. "Mizu!" he called out, feeling his heart break at the pained look on her face. "Mizu! It's Ian!"

Somewhere, deep within Mizu's mind, she sensed a familiarity. *Ian . . . That name . . . That face . . . But I have no recollection . . .*

Lance turned to the Creature. "Do your thing," he growled.

The Creature nodded and grinned sadistically. Pounding his fist into his hand, he swaggered forward. "You have not yet had the pleasure of battling me," he said in a *most* charming voice. In fact, it was so charming, so enchanting, that it nearly threw the group off guard. Helios's bow lowered slightly and the string slackened. Ian frowned, as he reminded himself why he was so angry. Even Evan, who had previously been experiencing a violent shaking in the Web of Life, was somehow less aware of it.

Dawn felt the hair on her arms stand up. *His voice . . . It is like a million lovely sounds, all mixed together. And yet there is a falseness to it, as though it were not a true sound at all, but rather something synthetic and fabricated.* She shook her head hard. "Your voice will hold no sway with us!" She stepped in front of Helios and Alan with determined look upon her face. "*You* have not yet had the pleasure of dealing with the Princess of Algernon. I do not take the kidnapping of my friend lightly."

Upon hearing Dawn's courageous words, the others doubled their efforts to shake away the hypnotic powers of the Creature's voice.

Undaunted, the Creature strode forward. "Darius, why are you hiding? I can see your essence wishes to come forward. How can a king like you hide behind the façade of such a boy? Are you really so very weak? Come on! You are a king! What does Kiara think of such behavior? Surely she is ashamed of her lover even more now than she was when you let her down in the past!"

Evan's eyes went wide and he fell to his knees clutching his head. "No . . ." he whispered, shaking from side to side. "Get away! Go back!"

"And you, Helios, or should I call you by your actual name, *Lord Robert*? Yes, it is true! You hide, just as Darius does, but use a hooded cloak and Vanishing Light magic instead of a pathetic body. Why is it that you can fight so well in battle, but are so poor at taking your heart's truest desire, hmmm? That desire being, of course, Princess Dawn. Why don't you take her, as you truly wish? Is that not why you joined her? Is that not why you follow her devotedly like a dog? It has really little to do with your parents' fate and you know it. You want Dawn, above all else in this world. You even tried to make Alan have a little accident back in the Tower of Fire, didn't you? I can see, even if Dawn can't. In truth, you are very, very selfish." The Creature's voice never faltered, nor hesitated for a moment. Helios—Lord Robert—grunted beneath his hood and joined Evan on the floor in a shaking heap.

Alan was growling and held up his dark crossbow. "You need to go back to the underworld where you belong! You are *nothing* more than a creation of Magica's spite!" But before he could fire, the Creature had begun speaking again.

"To the underworld? Shall I meet you there then? Seeing as we are both creatures filled with evil, I expect you will be there soon enough too." The Creature grinned maliciously. "Because of course, in the end, Dawn is going to purge the evil from you, which naturally will kill you in the process. It is an odd thing to love your executioner, isn't it? You know it very well. One of the Sisters told you the truth. I wonder how you can even look upon her face and not tremble at the pain she shall cause you. And I do find it rather amusing that you, a pitiful man who embraces the darkness, can even dare to love one so much higher than yourself. Though she is no prize, certainly Dawn is much too good for you. But you already knew that, didn't you?"

Alan's batwings flapped hard and he lolled to the side, dropping Queen L'eau and hitting his shoulder on the crystal wall, before slumping to the floor, head in his hands.

Dawn ran to Alan's side with a look of pure fire in her eyes. She glared at the Creature. "You monster! You and your forked tongue! You and your lies lies lies!" she screamed, feeling a deep fear at the words spoken to Alan. *How could I ever kill him? I simply could not!* "Don't you even *dare* pretend to know my mind! I will send you to the underworld in a million pieces!"

"Such big words, little princess. You try your best to be brave and responsible, when in reality you are still that spoiled, noisy child that Queen Alice worried herself sick over. You know my words ring true. Feel your heart tremble, Dawn! You do not truly have the confidence you pretend! Inside, you actually doubt everything about yourself, because you know you are faking it all! Every skill you have ever displayed was just acting! Imposter! Hear me! I see through you! I know the truth! I see you for what you truly are. You may have fooled others, but I have the gift of sight! Helpless, frightened, fraud! Look what you have brought your friends to! This is all your fault!"

Tears rolled down Dawn's face as she tried to fight off the wave of nausea that had overtaken her stomach. The Creature's words held a grain of truth—she really did lack complete confidence in her skills. No one would ever guess the deep fear she held in her heart, or so she thought, for Magica's Creature had seen her fear quite plainly.

Sensing his cousin about to go down, Ian stepped up. "Stop this nonsense right now! Even if you *can* see into our hearts, it means nothing! Do you hear me? Nothing at all! Everyone has their own private thoughts, fears, desires and battles! That is normal! None of us are perfect and we are all a little selfish and frightened sometimes. And yet that is what makes us unique! We—"

"Keep your self-righteous banter for someone with a soul to save," the Creature laughed. "You, Ian, are the worst of all!" he sneered, curling his lip. "You cannot fight to save your own life and your courage is severely lacking. Hiding behind your friends with a scroll and pen, that is your job. A sniveling scribe! A pansy bard! What good are you, really? What are your songs and tales and pretty face all worth? Think about this: you do not even have the ability to save the one you love. Yes, you do love her, I will give you that. But you don't deserve her, I can assure you of that too. How could you possibly think yourself worthy of an immortal Glintel? Hmmm? How could you place yourself so high . . . just like the vampire there. Your mother is a lowly peasant woman with a questionable reputation and your father, a pathetic prince who is afraid of his duties and instead digs in the dirt!"

Ian's face was like stone when he said, "I won't deny anything you have said, but whether I should or not, I love her. And, . . . perhaps I cannot save Mizu, as you say. But at the very least, I can die trying."

Mizu listened to all of this, in spite of the pain she was experiencing. In fact, it was this act that kept Mizu's mind separate from Nimue's and safe from Ralston's. By listening with all her heart and soul, Mizu was able to keep her mind to herself. Her empathy flowed like the water and for the first time in her life, she truly felt all range of human emotions. She saw deep feelings and fears laid bare. She saw great brave and strong people fall to their knees. She saw that everyone had weaknesses and yet . . . *we do not have to be ashamed of them! That blond boy . . . Ian . . . his words are so true. We are all a little scared sometimes and that is okay. As long as we press forward, it is okay. We must never stop and stagnate like a puddle of rancid water, for then we are filled with death. But if we keep moving and flowing like the mighty river, we soon pass over the rough areas and find calmer waters. Even though we know more rocks may come, we can survive them as long as we keep moving forward.*

With these thoughts in her mind, Mizu felt empowered, both physically and mentally. She felt fluid and light, like water itself. And with this feeling, she felt Nimue's righteous anger at what had been done to the world. Nimue herself seemed to have disappeared and was no longer pulling on Mizu's mind, rather, she flowed through Mizu's veins. Now, Mizu turned to Ralston, with the eyes of one who deserves retribution.

Lord Lance de Felda looked up at Mizu, floating in the air, and narrowed his eyes. *I have a feeling this is not going to go as planned. The Water Element has disappeared, meaning Mizu must have absorbed the spirit. As much as I hate it, I may have to leave this one for now. Blast! Nothing is going as I had planned! These Elementals are always one step ahead!*

Mizu raised her arms in a sort of ecstasy. "I *am* the Water! I am the flow of all things and the sum of all emotions!" She stared down at Ian and trembled slightly. "I am MIZU!" Her voice echoed off the crystal walls and Ian clenched his fists in determination.

"Mizu!" he cried out racing forward, but Magica's Creature stepped in front of him.

"Do not think you are capable of anything," the Creature sneered. "Worthless, spineless—"

He was cut off by Mizu's tremendous scream. "Hold your evil tongue! Your words mean NOTHING! You use them to gain energy from others, which they freely give up through their shame. But you will not have Ian, nor any of my other friends! Especially NOT Ian!" *I remember!*

The Creature rolled his eyes and looked to Ralston for direction or instruction, but Ralston was already gone. The Creature clenched his fists and seemed uncertain about what to do. He was, after all, technically unfinished and lacked a lot of the skills required for free will and independent thinking. Making a sound of disbelief, the Creature scowled and disappeared in a choking poof of toxic smoke.

With the Creature's departure, a cloud seemed to lift off of Dawn and the others, but shades of shame and embarrassment still hovered just below the surface. They refused to look each other in the eye and were all very silent. It was Mizu who broke the silence by gently alighting on the ground and transforming back into her original Glintel-made human clothing. She stepped forward softly before Ian and stared deeply into his blue eyes. "Ian . . ." she whispered and her voice was like the soft trickling of water.

Before Ian could reply, another voice, weak and faint, called out from behind Alan. Sitting daintily against the glimmering crystal wall was Queen L'eau, beautiful even as she lay dying. Mizu rushed to her side and the others, seemingly more aware now, gathered around the monarch. "Mizu," the Queen whispered as she reached up and touched the Glintel's cheek. "I never thought I would live to meet another like myself. All the years I felt so out of place and wrong." Her eyes looked suddenly fierce as she strained to look up. "But you must *never* feel that way, Mizu. You, we . . . are special. And love, true love, is never wrong. Never!" She coughed and looked weaker.

"Your Grace," Dawn said, kneeling beside the woman. "Let us take you from here and find aid."

The Queen smiled faintly. "No one can aid me now, even if they were willing. Ralston has turned the kingdom against my late husband and myself. There is no healer who would do me any good. It is at last time for me to return . . . to the sea."

Mizu started. "To the sea? What are you saying?"

Reaching out weakly, the Queen took Mizu's hand and squeezed it with all her strength. "I too, am a Glintel, Mizu. I too, took human shape and I too have always longed for the sea. Every minute of my waking life as a human, I have felt the pull of the sea. And yet, I resisted because I loved *him*." She said this with such passion that it was clear to anyone how much Queen L'eau had loved her husband. "He was my world while I was a human. No, it was not easy," she answered Mizu's unasked question. "But it was not wrong, either. Only positive energy comes from love and this world can use all it can get. I return to immortality and the sea with only the regret that I will not see my husband again. For where he goes, I cannot follow. The human afterlife is something I can never experience, which is why I am so grateful to have had earth." She gasped for breath and her grip slackened on Mizu's hand. "Can you now see how precious a gift it is for you to be human? What a precious experience this is for you? All the feelings and emotions you could never experience as a Glintel are now laid bare before you." She closed her eyes and sighed. "Nalopa is calling to me."

"Give her my love," Mizu whispered, gently kissing Queen L'eau on the forehead.

"Remember, Mizu. It is a precious gift . . . so rare . . . so . . . right."

With these words, Queen L'eau faded away from sight. There was nothing left to identify that a great Queen and Glintel had once been there. Mizu closed her eyes as two tears slid down her cheeks. Outside the cave entrance, a gentle rain was falling.

CHAPTER 13

Nissim's Decision

"**Y**OUR GRACES! WE CANNOT hold them back much longer!" a royal guard cried as he raced recklessly into the Great Hall.

Very little was left of Queen Alice and King Alexander's individual consciousnesses. Syoho and Otucu had almost completely taken over their bodies. Alice and Alexander stood in the center of the Great Hall, facing each other within a single pillar of white light. Oliver, Carrie, Nissim, Sparks and Wisp stood nearby looking grey and worn.

"What is the meaning of this?" demanded Oliver, feeling it was his duty to speak. His blue eyes looked as though all the life had been taken out of them and there was a soft touch of grey in his black hair.

"The people," the guard began, "they believe Queen Alice has betrayed them! They are trying to force down the main gate! It is sheer insanity! We cannot hold them off for long . . . it is the entire city!"

Oliver looked back towards Carrie who began to weep.

"What do they want?" Nissim asked, coming forward and placing a steadying hand upon Oliver's shoulder.

"Forgive me, my lord, but they want the Queen's head," the guard stuttered. "But we are loyal and will fight to our last breath to protect her!"

"Magica's cloud rains poison from the sky," Nissim sighed and truly looked his immense age. "It cannot be stopped and the Power forgive me, but I do not have enough magic left to help. I am old and tired, I admit at last."

"My lord, is there nothing we can do to prevent them from desecrating our Queen?" asked the guard desperately. He and his army were loyal to King Alexander and had served in the castle for many decades. He would not allow such dishonor to come upon the Queen if he could help it. "Tell me, wizard, what can we do?"

Nissim looked sad but said, "We could implore the goddess Syoho to let the dark dome fall."

The guard looked upon Alice and Alexander within the pillar of light. "They are all that prevents us from instant destruction?" he asked.

Nissim nodded slowly. "They love the people of this city so . . ."

"Make them let go!" the guard suddenly cried out desperately. "To save you all from a horrible end, make them let go! Let us all fall with honour! Please, I beg you! You do not know what they will do to her!"

"Nissim . . ." Oliver spoke up and looked at the wizard. "I will not let them hurt Carrie or my sister." There was a look of determination that Nissim had never see on Oliver's face.

A loud scream down the hall signaled that the people had broken through the main gate.

"My men!" cried the guard falling to his knees. "They are coming! What will it be, wizard? They will tear you to pieces too!"

Wisp, the Pegasus-Unicorn, softy approached Nissim with Sparks the fairy perched on her forehead, holding onto her horn. "Nissim," Sparks said tearfully, "let's give all our energy to Dawn. She is the world's hope now."

Wisp nodded. "It is of better use to her. Let Alice use our energy in the way she sees fit."

The rumbling down the halls was louder now. Soon the mob would make their way into the Great Hall.

"Alice's mother died here in this chamber, in the most hideous of ways." Nissim spoke quietly and then more loudly, "I will not allow Alice the same fate!" He went to stand before the pillar of light. Falling to one knee he said, "Great Syoho and Otucu. Hear me! Let the dark dome fall! Let it go! Alice! We offer ourselves to Dawn!"

The figure who was mostly Syoho, but partially Alice, nodded her head. "You have asked and the Goddess hears. So be it." A tear rolled down her cheek.

* * *

"By the Power!" exclaimed Cloud Li as he looked down upon Fadreama. Queen Kiraku was by his side as they watched the dark dome over Devona implode upon itself. It was instantaneous destruction. "No one could have survived that . . ." Cloud Li whispered.

"She let it go," Kiraku said softly. "Syoho let it go."

"So this is really it, then," Cloud Li sighed. "Fadreama truly is dying. With the grace of Syoho gone . . . it cannot be much longer."

"Princess Dawn is still down there," Kiraku pointed out. "I do not know what she can do, but perhaps . . . I don't know."

Cloud Li put his arm around Kiraku and held her close. "Ah Nissim, you finally join your brother." He shook his head. "We in the Cloud Realm will go on, but I sometimes wonder . . . is it a blessing or a curse?"

*   *   *

Queen Alexandria screamed like a woman who has gone completely mad. She fell to the floor in her throne room sobbing and beating the ground wildly with her fists.

Two of the Queen's ladies raced to her side and tried to restrain her. "Someone help before she hurts herself! We must get her to her chamber!" one of the ladies exclaimed. The Queen's physician and several servants rushed forward to assist the ladies.

"What is going on?" asked Lady Harmony, as she appeared in the doorway.

Everyone looked up, including the Queen and there was silence all around. "Your Grace!" Harmony ran towards her mother-in-law. Taking the woman's hands she said, "It's . . . Fadreama, isn't it?"

"Sweet Harmony," Queen Alexandria said through tears and sobs. "You have escaped much in your life . . . and you have escaped yet again."

"Tell me! What has happened!" Harmony cried, gripping the Queen's sleeve.

"Devona and all who live there . . . gone!" She lapsed into inaudible wails and Harmony was pushed back by servants.

"Alice . . ." Harmony stood very still as she whispered her best friend's name. The sheer enormity of this revelation nearly knocked the life out of her. "Evan . . ."

Turning on her heels, Harmony raced out of the throne room. She found Andre lounging on his wicker chair in the garden, as usual. She reached him huffing and puffing out of breath. Looking up, Andre said, "What on earth is the matter with you?"

Her lip trembled as she stood staring at her husband, a man she hardly knew anymore, if she knew him at all. Then, Harmony threw herself into his arms and cried.

Surprised and unnerved, for a moment Andre did not know how to react. Then sensing something odd, Andre sat up straighter and put his arms around Harmony. "Tell me, what has happened?"

"Devona . . . is gone! Completely gone! There is nothing left!" she cried.

It took a moment for the implications of this information to sink in. Paling, Andre whispered, "And the people?"

"Gone! Alice! Alexander! Evan! Everyone!" Harmony screamed.

Andre felt as though he had been slapped across the face. It was well that he was sitting, for he likely would have fainted. *My brother . . . My son . . . Alice . . .* Tightening his lips he pulled Harmony closer and buried his face in her red hair.

CHAPTER 14

Of Truth and Lies

Flow like the WATER,
But don't crash like the wave,
For with too much force, no one can be saved.

WORDS ECHOED IN THE depths of Mizu's soul. She stood under the overhang of an abandoned villager's house. The roof was rotting and moss grew all over, but it was the best shelter the group could find under the circumstances. Gentle rain filled the air with a heavy sweetness stirred up from the vegetation on the forest floor. As Mizu stared out into the dawn, she could not tell what season it was anymore. Everything had sort of flowed into one state of being and she had a difficult time knowing what was real and what was imagined.

The Water . . . she is inside me now—a part of my soul, just as the Fire is a part of Evan. It is an unsettling feeling, all that raw power. It scares me just a little. I never know when it is going to suddenly burst free and I know even less what that power will do, for I have no control over the element. I am just a protector, a shell, a carrier. And when the end comes . . . what then? She sighed and held her arms tightly.

"It is a little refreshing, is it not?" came a voice from behind.

Mizu started and turned around. "What?"

"The rain," Ian nodded. "It is rather refreshing after everything."

"After everything . . ." Mizu repeated quietly. "What are we going to do?"

"You mean 'we' as a group, or 'we' as in *you and me*?" Ian touched Mizu's shoulder and slipped his arm around her. She relaxed under his protection.

"You make me feel safe, Ian," Mizu smiled. "I know you aren't really a warrior or anything, but just your presence calms me. That's not to say we both wouldn't die if we were attacked," she joked softly.

Ian laughed a little. "I can't argue with that, but you need to know that I would try and protect you nonetheless."

Mizu smiled and leaned closer. "I know you would. But I would protect you too. You have . . . made me care too much."

"My Mizu," Ian whispered. "My beautiful, irreplaceable, special Mizu. There is no one in the world quite like you, nor will there ever be again."

"There have been other Glintels turned human before," Mizu whispered sadly. "But I do not think there will be any to follow me, not because they choose not to, but rather, because this is the end."

Ian did not respond, but merely held Mizu tightly, with a grim look set across his handsome features.

* * *

Kiara observed this exchange from the nearby bushes along with Chartreuse, who for reasons Kiara could not derive, was following her.

"A grim couple, are they not," Kiara remarked quietly, her pale skin dewy from the rain.

"Realistic," Chartreuse replied with a slight smile.

"Why are you following me around anyway?" she asked with slight annoyance.

"We are travelling in the same direction for the moment," Chartreuse replied lightly. "Does it bother you, honey?" She laughed in her peculiar way.

"Quiet down," Kiara scolded sulkily. *I really can't believe this giant is a woman!*

Chartreuse's face softened. "Do you honestly think to win Darius back? That story was written long ago and the book closed. Things were very different back then, very different indeed."

"You speak as though you were there," Kiara commented while eyeing Chartreuse carefully. "I don't fully understand your motives."

"Nor will you ever, my dear. I am an enigma." Chartreuse paused and added, "Let's just say Ralston and I go way back. I want to see how this will end and if I will have any part in it."

* * *

Dawn, Alan, Evan and Robert were sitting before the abandoned hearth in the villager's house. A fire crackled and smoked with the damp wood they had used to start it. As a result, a rather sickly scent hung in the air and clung to the rafters. There was a tense silence woven in with the smoke and it hung just as heavily. Each person was engrossed in the horrid memory of the Creature's words. There had been a note of truth in the accusations he had made and now that there was a lull in the action, everyone was thinking and searching their own soul.

Dawn wrung her hands together nervously. *What can I say? What can I do? Can things ever be the same again? Stop! It was all lies, wasn't it?* Her heart whispered faintly. *No, he merely took a small piece of truth and . . . and . . .* "And I don't know what!" she suddenly found herself on her feet and screaming.

Three male faces turned to stare at her in wonderment. "Dawn?" Alan asked with concern and then suddenly blushing, looked at his feet.

"I can't stand this!" Dawn cried in frustration, stamping her foot. "Look what *they* have reduced us to!"

"Dawn . . ." Evan's voice cracked as he tried to speak.

"His words are poison and we are succumbing to it!" Dawn continued, fighting back her own emotions. "We need to somehow rise above it . . . But why should you listen to me anyway? I usually just fake courage." She collapsed back down on the floor before the fire.

For a moment, no one moved. Only the sound of rain on the roof could be heard. And then it was Alan who finally found the courage to move. He knelt on the floor before Dawn and swallowed hard. *I don't care what that monster said. He does NOT know my heart. No one can know my own heart but me! I will not give him such a privilege!* He reached out and gently put his hand under Dawn's chin and raised her face to look at him. He took a deep breath. "You are what holds all our hearts together, Dawn. It is your pure love for . . . everything, that keeps us going each day. You show us truly what it is to be brave. With all that has happened, with all you have endured and continue to endure each day, you are the model of bravery. We . . . I, would never have made it this far without you. You saved me from my own darkness, Dawn. And in the end, even if that darkness swallows me, at least I was able to spend some time in the light."

Dawn's eyes brightened and seemed to gain a spark which glowed and illuminated the young man before her. "Alan, I will *never* give you up to the darkness. I do not care what anyone says or thinks or predicts. I know your heart and it is *good*. I will *save* you, Alan, not destroy you. I will not let you go into the dark, I promise."

Her eyes were so earnest that Alan could not help but believe the words she said. And for the first time in a long time, he felt the foreign sensation known as *hope*. Without thinking, he clasped Dawn's hand and whispered, "I know, Dawn. I *know.*"

Helios—Lord Robert—watched this exchange with a mixture of sorrow, regret, shame and jealousy. His heart ached like he never knew it could and he wanted nothing more than to bury his face far away from the light. *What do they think of me now? No longer the mysterious Vanishing Light, I am nothing but a man with some skill granted by Nissim. I didn't even earn my abilities. And my motives are selfish indeed, because I am doing it to win Dawn. That is all I ever wanted. Not noble at all. Even the vampire is more noble than I. Perhaps I truly did send him to his death in the Tower . . .*

Dawn watched the man she had previously known as Helios. He seemed so deeply ashamed and upset. It hurt her heart to see him in such a state. *I still remember the awe I felt for him when we first danced at my birthday ball. He is still that noble warrior that he has always been. If only I can make him see that he truly is worthy.* With Alan's help, she got to her feet and made her way over to the shadows. With one hand, she gently pulled Robert into the firelight. At her touch, Robert felt electrified and warm—it was the birthday ball all over again, the night he fell in love with her.

Looking at his face, no longer covered by a shroud, Dawn said, "You have a very handsome face, Lord Robert. I am glad to see it in the open now. I have missed you greatly and now I realize that you have never left my side."

"Dawn . . . how can you even bear to look at me with all that I have done?"

"With all you have done? Why, Lord Robert, you have done so much good! We never could have won so many battles without you by our sides. You have been indispensible to us, even if we were not aware it was you," Dawn explained in all honesty. Evan nodded in agreement and Alan made a slightly distracted noise.

"But, Dawn, my motives were so *impure.*" He looked nervously at Alan. "I have loved you from the very first moment I heard your name. Then when I finally met you, I felt I had been swept away by your beauty and innocent heart. I was and remain, devoted to you and solely you. Everything I do . . . it is not for my parents, nor for the kingdom or even Fadreama. It is all for *you.* And perhaps, just as Alan feels, I am not worthy of you at all. Though my deeds may seem positive, my motivation is so selfish that it defeats the effort."

"You are wrong, Robert," Dawn whispered intensely. She stared deeply into Robert's eyes and felt the same attraction she had felt on the night of their first dance—though it was somehow diminished and innocent now. Her feelings for Alan seemed to hold her very soul. "You may think you do it purely for me, but Robert, you have a good heart, I know this. Never think your good works are in vain. And if you have a side motive, well, you are a man, Robert." She paused and added, "The very fact that you are aware of your thoughts and question them, indicates that you are good. You have a conscience. Only truly wicked people lack a conscience. That is what separates us from them. They never question themselves."

Robert smiled at this and felt significantly kinder towards himself. His motives did not change, but he began to feel that it was okay to have such thoughts. Slowly he reached out and embraced Dawn tightly, much to Alan's chagrin. "Thank you, my princess. I am forever devoted to you and whatever cause you take up."

As he released her from his warm embrace, Dawn blushed fiercely and noticed Alan's clenched fists. Gently she touched his hands and felt them relax. Looking over at Evan, she asked, "Cousin, are you managing? You have been awfully quiet."

Evan poked at the fire with a stick, sending tiny sparkling embers into the air. The Fire in his blood responded with a pulse. "The Creature did not insult me. In fact, he ignored my presence altogether, which I suppose is kind of an insult in itself." Poking more violently at the fire, Evan continued, "The Creature spoke directly to Darius and certainly he made the late king angry. Darius is extremely upset and ashamed right now. His frustration flows through me and it is like a toxin. But . . . I will not . . . let him out. I fear what he may do. He is just so very, very angry." *Should I tell them that Kiara is nearby? No . . . I think she will not approach this time.*

The others nodded sympathetically, though they could never fully understand how torn Evan felt. "You are right to contain him," Robert spoke up. "King Darius is not of this era. His time has passed, though so long as Kiara walks, he will never rest."

"Unless I die," Evan said ruefully. "And then, what becomes of us both? We are the same soul, so do our consciousnesses merge or what? Does Evan still exist? Does Darius? What about all the other hundreds of lives my soul has endured before Darius? Where are they now? Are we really lost after this life? Do our loves fade into the abyss? Can any of us honestly say to someone, 'I will love you forever'?"

"Those are some awfully deep questions you are pondering," Ian commented from the doorway. Mizu stood beside him, clutching his hand shyly. "Some things are best left alone, or left at least to the bards."

Evan suddenly laughed. "I think you are right, my friend. We have more important issues to discuss."

"Like what exactly are we going to do next?" Mizu piped up. "There are two elements left at Crystal Points—the Air and the Earth. We all know that means Ian and Alan."

"Exactly," Evan nodded. "Ralston will be attempting something, though I think he may be changing his strategies somehow. He has lost two elements already and I doubt he wants to lose the next two so easily."

"I can't help but wonder if he knows about the great purification that is supposed to happen when we absorb all the elements. Chartreuse said that if Ralston were to somehow gain control of all the elements, he would have the power to instantly absorb all the Fragments of Cardew at once," Robert mused.

"How would he have such knowledge?" Dawn asked. "We don't even know exactly how to purify the land and we are the ones who must do it. No, I think Ralston does not know what will happen if he should fail. He may perhaps fear it, but he does not know. Of this, I am fairly certain."

"He did know that I was the protector of water," Mizu put forth.

"I'm sure anyone could have guessed that," Ian laughed.

She gave him a playful slap in the arm. "What I mean is, does he know the remaining elements? Does he know about Ian, Alan and Dawn?"

"That is something I do not know," Dawn admitted, running her fingers anxiously through her glittering hair. Throughout everything it had never lost its fairy shimmer. She sat down on a creaking old chair. "I don't know what we should do or where we should go. I wish I could tell you, but I have no idea. Time is so short . . . We cannot afford to go the wrong direction and make a mistake."

Outside, the sky was churning with the rainclouds. Then suddenly, cutting through the grey, came a single beam of light. It shot through the air and into a crack on the villager's thatched roof. The beam of light landed directly in the center of the confused group of friends.

"What on earth?" Alan exclaimed as Dawn jumped to her feet and screamed, tears suddenly running down her cheeks. She fell to her knees and cried, "Mother!"

CHAPTER 15

Alice Speaks

"**Y**OUR GRACE!" LORD ROBERT was on his knees in an instant. With a bowed head, he trembled at what this apparition could mean. *Surely it does not mean that Devona is completely lost . . . that the Queen, for all her efforts, is . . .*

The translucent image of Queen Alice, in all her beauty and magnificence did indeed stand in the center of the crumbling and leaking hut. Alice glowed and pulsated with a light that radiated from beyond the world of Fadreama. Her lovely eyes were sad though and rested solely on Dawn.

"My daughter," she whispered, "all that I left to the world."

"Left to the world?" Evan whispered, jumping to his feet.

"Your Grace? What has happen—" With a grunt, he fell to the floor in a cold sweat. Gasping for breath he whispered, "T . . . the Web. What . . ." *This pain . . . May the Power help us all!*

"So now you feel the vibration. It has finally reached this part of Fadreama. Syoho let go. She let go of the dark dome over Devona. She has withdrawn her support from this world. I could not convince her otherwise. She said . . . it was time." Alice's eyes held such sadness . . . It was heartbreaking to see the once mighty queen.

"Devona then," Ian began quietly, "and all those within it, are gone." *My dear parents. My poor mother. And my father . . . I cannot blame him for this. Not this time.*

Dawn began to shake and Alan immediately put his arm around her, while trying not to show his own pain, for indeed, he felt the loss. Through this sadness came an anger that stirred his vampire blood. It was a stirring which called out for not revenge, but rather, justice and . . . reckoning.

Evan's chest tightened as the Web shook. *What of my parents in the fairy realm of Alexandria? I think I will never see them again, but at least they will go on living . . . I cannot imagine my mother's sorrow though. She must be devastated . . . And grandmother . . . Perhaps they think I am dead too . . .*

"Mother, mother," Dawn cried, unable to utter another word. Everything she had ever known was gone and could never be brought back. This could not be fixed, or repaired by any means of magic. *Truly,* she thought, *revolution is here and it shall leave nothing in its wake but tragedy. When will I be able to lay down my weapons and finally be free of all this madness?*

Alice reached a hand out towards her daughter, but she could not touch her. They were no longer within the same world and would never be again. Then, remembering why she was appearing, Alice spoke softly but with strength, "Dawn, Dawn, you must listen carefully to me now. Though my part is over, yours, I'm afraid, is not. You cannot rest until you finish what you have started, no matter how difficult it becomes." A tear slipped from the corner of her eye and landed with a 'ping' on the ground.

Dawn finally found the courage to look up at her mother's face. "I don't know what to do anymore! I am so tired of these battles! I hardly even recognize myself anymore! What have I become?"

"You are more than yourself, Dawn," Alice replied. "You are so much to so many and you will do great things before the end. You are the very soul of Fadreama and you are about to shout 'enough is enough' to the parasites which have infested the land." Her eyes sparked suddenly. "When the time comes, do not hesitate. It is the right thing to do."

"I am still confused, Mother! I do not know what you mean!" Dawn pleaded tearfully. "Where do we go? What do we do? I beg you! Please! Help us!"

"Ralston can *never* control the elements. He can control the people who guard Crystal Points, or perhaps the country each lies within. But he can never truly hold a Crystal Point within his grasp. It is simply an impossibility. By now he will have figured this out. So now that he cannot possess the elements, he will work to prevent you from gaining anymore. The Air and the Earth await in the west. You must go to them and absorb them." She looked at Ian and Alan. "Once the element is within you, it is safe and stable . . . but not balanced." Alice looked troubled and her image trembled slightly.

"So how do we create the balance, Mother?" asked Dawn getting to her feet and trying desperately to grasp at some sort of inner strength.

Alice looked intently at Dawn and replied, "You must destroy Fadreama. You must purify it completely, which will tear it to pieces."

There was a collective gasp and then heavy silence in the room after Alice spoke these dreadful words. Swallowing hard, Evan stepped up and asked, "Is there any other way?" His eyes were glassy with tears.

Alice shook her head sadly. "No. There is no other way. We have tried and tried to save this land but it has only become progressively worse. Now the land has been thrown into turmoil by the lies whispered by Ralston Radburn through the lips of my poor cousin, Lance. It is time to end all of this suffering for everyone." She looked carefully at Dawn. "For everyone."

Dawn nodded slowly and tried to sound brave. "I understand now, Mother." Tears rolled down her cheeks and she took a great breath. "It will be time soon to say goodbye. If I must carry this burden . . . then so be it."

"But what of the other worlds? What of Alexandria and the Cloud Realm?" asked Evan unable to hold his peace any longer. *Yet another person I failed to protect. Mother . . . Cassandra . . . Kiara . . .*

"They will be spared, because they are no longer connected to Fadreama, but there will never be any way to access them again. Your mother, my dearest friend Harmony . . . she will go on in Alexandria." Yet another tear fell from Alice's eye and landed on the floor with a tiny tinkle.

Evan stood motionless for a moment and then merely closed his eyes and nodded. *At least, she will live.* He pulled the pain deep within himself and shoved it somewhere behind Daris who was looking on in wonderment. Inside Evan's soul, Darius looked upon Queen Alice and realized that this was his own mother reincarnated and now passed on again. He thought of how he had failed her by dying and leaving his frail younger brother in charge. And now Evan felt that he had failed his own mother too. It was the first feeling that actually connected their hearts together.

Mizu laced her arm through Ian's and held him tightly, as he silently reeled from the death of his parents.

Robert too had now lost both parents, as his mother had been recovering in Dalton Castle which now no longer existed. *And so it truly is over. Nissim had given me reason to believe we had hope, but now . . .*

As if reading Robert's thoughts, Alice said, "Our good Nissim is gone. Everyone gave everything they possibly could to save Devona, but in the end, it was not enough. I am so sorry, Dawn."

"No, Mother!" Dawn exclaimed. "This is not your fault! It is no one's fault. This is just the way it is and we must do our best as long as we can."

Alice gazed with pride upon her daughter. *We made you, Alex and I. Syoho had nothing to do with this!* "And now, you must go to Florian and Ian must absorb the Air. Then to Bainbridge for Alan to take the Earth. The Crystal Points in these two countries are very near to each other. You must beware of Ralston's traps, for he knows you will be going there. He has only one directive now: to kill you all. If he cannot have the elements, he can only hope to kill those who can. He will stop at nothing. You are all in grave danger, but especially Ian and Alan." Alice was very solemn.

"Is there a way to travel faster than with the Diamond Roses?" asked Dawn.

"Look to the ground," Alice whispered. "Those two tiny teardrops—hold them together in your hands and see what happens. But I can linger no longer. The Lady has called me back and this time it is to stay. Syoho gets her life back . . . at the cost of mine."

"Mother! Will I ever see you again?" Dawn cried with passion.

Alice could not speak—the pain was far too great. She merely shook her head 'no'. "I made this contract long ago. We must go to different places, my darling. But know this, there was never a prouder mother than I to have had such a daughter. Remember that. No matter what happens, remember that. You have made my human life worthwhile, Dawn. You and I will make Syoho remember that for all eternity. Though 'Alice' may be gone, that feeling will stay within the goddess forever and though she may not understand it, she will know it comes from Alice."

Trying to be strong, Dawn smiled. "I will not fail you. When I leave, Fadreama will be pure, I promise you that."

"I knew that you would," Alice smiled and began to fade.

"Find some happiness before the end." These were her last words and Queen Alice faded back into the eternal mind of Syoho, never to walk the earth again.

CHAPTER 16

Ralston Strikes Back

RALSTON RADBURN WAS LIVID, furious and every other possible description of enraged. His—that is, Lance's—body was tense with pent up anger and frustration. A large blue vein throbbed above his left eye, marring the handsome face of Lord Lance de Felda. He was on the border of Florian, which was the most westerly land in all of Fadreama.

It was a country of beautiful grassy meadows, filled with an abundance of flowers and green lawns. The sky was, more often than not, blue in this land and crystal clear. The people were of an intellectual and artistic nature. They valued storytelling, music making and art above all else. The physical build of the Florians reflected their values, for they were thin and graceful with an eloquence of movement. Their flare for sculpture was evident in the great columned pavilions which dotted the landscape, as well as dominated the cities and towns. If any land had been made for Ian, it was Florian. Thus, it was fitting that the element Air had chosen this place for its Crystal Point stronghold in the great Meadow of Winds. Ian's sacred charge, the Air, was calling out to him from the city of Dale. Its vibrations shook the atmosphere so hard that even Ralston could sense it.

Ralston clenched his fists and brought them down hard upon the wooden bar table before him. He sat cloaked in a pub, located in an obscure little border village, with the Creature as his only companion. "Though the Earth Crystal Point is closer, it is the Air that calls out," he mused angrily. "Surely the one among Dawn's companions who is bound to Air will be drawn to the call."

"Do you know which among them is the guardian of Air?" asked the Creature.

"Going merely by archetypes, it must be Ian, son of that pansy Prince Edric and his tempting blond wife, Carrie. Pity for Lord Lance that she had to be destroyed in Devona along with the others." Ralston shook his head. "Ian has all the right characteristics for Air and would fit perfectly with the artsy people in Florian." Ralston considered for another moment with a scowl upon his features. "Yes, I am certain it is Ian."

"So what's your plan then?" asked the Creature, eager for information.

Ralston leaned back upon his chair and looked frustrated. "I could take over the Crystal Point by deceiving those ninnies in Florian, but what would that achieve? NOTHING! I have done it twice with no results!" The other pub patrons paused in their drinks to look over at Ralston and raise an eyebrow. He lowered his voice and continued, "It seems I cannot absorb the element itself. Our energies are somehow . . . incompatible. And neither can I absorb the person who takes the element within their soul. Again, it is incompatible." He would not say 'their power is too great'. No, that would be far too much for Ralston to believe.

"That leaves you in quite the position," the Creature commented neutrally.

"Indeed it does," Ralston hissed again. "There seems to be only one course of action. It does not grant me any extra power, but it does diminish that of the elements and leaves two of them unprotected. It is quite basic in theory, but may prove difficult in action. However, I think we can manage it well enough if we pool all our resources." Ralston clasped his hands tightly together. "We will kill the guardians who have yet to absorb an element and naturally anyone else we possibly can. If I cannot have the Elemental power, then I will ensure that no one else can either."

The Creature nodded admiringly. "A very good plot indeed." His eyes glistened darkly. "Very good indeed."

* * *

Ian began to sing a song—one that he had never heard before. The group was sitting around a campfire at the intersection of the Arianrod and Taliesin Rivers, just outside of Hedwig. They were debating about which direction they should take, in order to avoid Ralston and his minions. Yet how had they gone so far so quickly?

Flashback

"These teardrops," Dawn whispered holding the two crystals gently in her hand, "there is something special about them." One glittered a rose coloured hue and their other shimmered crystal clear. "They must be Elf Stones," she whispered.

"Are you certain?" asked Evan, coming in for a closer look. He inspected the two glittering jewels in Dawn's palm. "They are so perfect . . . I do believe they are more beautiful than any of your other Elf Stones."

"They are Elf Stones, I know," Dawn affirmed. "I can feel it in my heart and soul. No one but myself could have received these stones. They did not exist until now. This is further proof that Syoho is a part of everyone—both humans and the Acjah. We are all part of the same world and governed by the same forces. Ignatius may have believed himself to have given me a weapon of the Acjah, but it is really just like any other."

"Well, I wouldn't go *that* far," Mizu smiled gently. "I doubt your Acjah friends would appreciate being lumped in with the human or even Glintel world, for that matter."

Alan now came to stand beside Dawn. As he peered at the glittering stones he wondered, "But what do they do? Surely they are directly related to our quest. That is why the Queen appeared here just now. It had to have been her last gift."

Dawn brought forth the Light of the Earth. Both stones easily found their way into an indentation on the handle. Holding the torch above her head, Dawn closed her eyes and whispered, "Rose."

There was a flash of pink light and the rose coloured stone appeared to hover at the top of the torch. "It is an eternal Diamond Rose stone," Dawn whispered, as the answer seemed to flow from the stone to her lips. It will transport us anywhere we desire directly."

"Amazing," breathed Lord Robert.

With a worried expression, Alan squeezed Dawn's arm. "But at what price? Remember, the power of these stones flows from you. If you transport all of us a great distance, you will be left in a weakened state."

"That's right, Dawn," Evan agreed. "Remember when you used the Time Stone? Alan had to hold you up. This stone seems like it would utilize a lot of your strength. Just look at what happens to a regular Diamond Rose after it is used—it turns to dust! With this stone, it will be your own powers giving it support."

Dawn bit her lip tensely. *They are right, of course. If I use this stone—which I must—then I will be useless when we arrive at our destination. Why must magic always exact such a price?* She shook her head defiantly. "But we have no choice."

"She is right," Mizu nodded. "We do have no choice. There are two elements left to be protected and very little time to be spent on travelling. Fadreama is wide . . . this is our only choice. We have no Diamond Roses left."

"We will do what we must, come what may. We shall deal with my weakness when it happens," Dawn agreed. "For now, we need to get away from here. Pick a location that is near, but not quite at the next Crystal Point. We need time to think."

Without hesitation, Lord Robert spoke up, "Hedwig—on the outskirts of the city, where the great rivers intersect."

Dawn nodded and the Rose Stone glowed.

End Flashback

Ian was singing a song he had never heard before. His lips had just suddenly started to move and the lyrics had entered his mind unbidden.

> *"Fly high like the AIR,*
> *But don't destroy like the gale.*
> *For the seduction of power,*
> *Will cause you to fail."*

The others in the group simply stared at their friend, for his melodious voice had started up out of nowhere.

"Ian, are you okay?" Mizu asked, her face filled with emotion and concern.

As though awakening from a daze, Ian shook his head hard. Then, with glassy eyes, he gave a weak smile to the others. "The element of Air has just called out. Can you imagine the feeling? He actually called out to me. His name is Paralda."

"Paralda . . ." Mizu repeated slowly.

"Paralda . . ." Evan also whispered.

Inside these two, the elements of Fire and Water recognized the name of their companion. Dijin and Nimue knew the power of that name.

"I know that the Earth's Crystal Point is closer in Bainbridge, but I feel that the Air needs me now," Ian explained with pleading eyes. He could feel the urgency coming from Paralda and also the warning of danger.

"The Earth says nothing to me, even though I am supposedly its protector," Alan confirmed. "I say we go where we are needed." He was kneeling protectively beside the sleeping form of Dawn, who was curled up in a blanket on the ground. The sheer force of using the Rose Stone had knocked her out cold. Alan furrowed his brows. "But getting to Florian may be trouble for poor Dawn."

Jealously Robert watched Alan care for the Princess. His heart ached bitterly. Robert's love for Dawn had not diminished, despite where the bulk of her affections lay. "Alan is right. The Rose Stone is far too much for Dawn to continue using."

"There is little time," Ian pressed. "Paralda says there is danger on the horizon. Ralston is on the move again."

"Dawn is not such a weakling!" Mizu suddenly declared with passion. Her eyes seemed to roar like the ocean waves. If the Acjah entrusted her with the Light of the Earth, then she is fully capable of using it repeatedly! If Queen Alice—the Goddess Syoho—deemed Dawn capable of having the Rose Stone, then Dawn must be able! The powers that be never give us anything we cannot handle! Everything they ask of us they know we can manage, however difficult it may seem at the time! We must place some faith in Dawn's power and trust her!"

"Thank you . . . Mizu . . ." Dawn whispered, opening her eyes and slowly sitting up with Alan's aid.

"I am okay, Alan," she said with a soft smile that penetrated Alan's darkness straight to his human heart. Though he wanted to turn away, he found that her eyes mesmerized his and he allowed himself to enjoy it.

Dawn turned to Ian as she got to her feet. "It is Florian then that we must travel to?"

He nodded. "Paralda says we must hurry. The dark forces are becoming desperate and moving quickly."

"Ralston is at his wit's end, I should think," Evan mused and then tensed as he felt the Web of Life tremble as darkness slithered along its strands. Both Dijin and Darius called a warning, but it was too late.

"Being at my wit's end is where I fight best though," came a voice from the air. A sudden blast of icy wind sent the group flying backwards through the forest.

When the fog had cleared Evan looked over at his companions, doing a quick mental check that everyone was okay.

"Is everyone alri . . ." his voice trailed off when he saw the giant spear protruding from Ian's chest.

CHAPTER 17

Fighting For Air

EVERYTHING SEEMED TO BE in slow motion. Ian had felt himself falling backwards to the ground, even before he realized what had just occurred. He landed hard on his back and within seconds, Mizu was at his side, cradling his head and looking absolutely frantic.

What is it she is saying? he wondered vaguely, still not fully aware of his surroundings. Sounds seemed to be muffled, as though he were under water and though his vision was fine, everything did seem slower. Oddly enough, he felt absolutely no pain.

Mizu touched the side of Ian's face and looked intently at him, while mouthing some words he could neither hear, nor understand. She squeezed his hand, while her lips kept moving.

She is so beautiful, Ian thought to himself. *Why does she look so afraid? Her eyes are filled with terror and panic.* And then she suddenly shook Ian's hand and seemed to be screaming. Ian watched all this from his vantage point behind Evan, who was putting his weight on Ian's chest. Evan was holding a wadded up cloth—a great strip of Mizu's dress—on Ian's chest. Ian gasped a little when he realized the cloth was soaked in blood. *My blood . . . ?* He was very confused. *Why am I here? Why am I standing here, when I am lying there?*

Mizu seemed to be screaming and Dawn put her arms around the Glintel and mouthed something in her ear, but Mizu seemed unable to listen. She shook violently and threw her head backwards in agony. Sweat glistened on Evan's brow as he put pressure on the bloody cloth. Alan and Robert stood beside Evan, seemingly uncertain of what to do, though both their eyes expressed the same emotion: defeat.

What has happened to me . . . ? Ian continued to take in the scene before him but it wavered before his eyes. *This can't be real . . . That is me on the ground, surrounded by everyone. That is my blood on Mizu's dress and yet here I stand, though no one seems to notice.* Ian seemed unable to draw the obvious conclusion.

And then a great wind swept by. It sang out to him in the voice of Selene, one of the Three Sisters they had met in Algernon. "You must live," she called out, her voice carried high upon the wind. "You, above all else must survive! Someone has to tell the tale. Someone has to pass on the truth! Hear me, Ian! You must live!"

These words resounded around Ian and he suddenly knew that only he could hear them, for he now understood that he was outside of his body. Ian stood at the very brink of death. The silver cord which connects soul to body had not yet been severed—only stretched. His life could now go either way, though he knew that somehow he needed to live. He needed to get back inside his body and breathe the air.

But wait! Ralston is still here! He stands gloating in the distance! What will we do? There is little time!

Then, like a great blast from a hurricane, came the voice of Paralda. Ian could not mistake the voice of his patron element. "Come to Florian!" instructed the Air. "Now! They can heal you! They can save you! You must live! Ask for Alethea! She will save you! Then you must save me! You, Ian, do not get the easy way out. You must live." The wind blew harder and Ian felt himself violently flying through the air. Great pain swept over him as he felt himself crashing back into the confines of flesh and bone.

Gasping for air, Ian now felt the burning and tearing pain that could only mean he was in grave danger. He could feel the sweat on his face as he tried with difficulty to breathe.

"He has opened his eyes!" Mizu screamed in a hysterical voice.

"Florian . . ." Ian murmured. He could barely find enough breath to speak. "Take us . . . Florian . . . Alethea, find." It was torture to manage these words.

"What?" Mizu managed through her tears. "Florian? Alethea?"

"Ralston watches us yet," Robert observed. "He watches to see that the deed is done." Turning to Alan, Robert now said, "I think you are also in danger."

Alan grimaced. "Let him try."

"Not now!" Dawn exclaimed. "I know what Ian means!" *I felt it in my heart when the wind blew by.* "I must use my new Elf Stone to transport us directly to Florian. The name Ian whispered—Alethea—I think she alone can heal such a grievous wound. *Though I know not how. One of Ian's lungs is gone and by the amount of blood, I'd say his heart has been damaged.* Her stomach clenched. *I must find the strength to do this! Please, cousin, hold onto life!*

Both Alan and Robert declared a passionate 'No!' at the same time.

"Dawn, you just used the stone recently and it drained you. Is it wise—" she interrupted Robert.

"I understand you are trying to protect me, but in war there is no time for such thoughts. Look, Ralston is just standing there! He could kill us all in an instant. We must outwit him and be faster! We must go now!" With these words she rapidly released the Light of the Earth and had the Rose Stone called forth before anyone knew what had happened. With the regal command of authority in her voice and an expression of determination reminiscent of Alice, Dawn declared, "Rose Stone! Take us to Alethea in Florian, NOW!"

Such energy poured out of Dawn that it took everyone by surprise. White light lit up the forest, bending the trees nearly to their breaking point. The sky shone as though Dawn's light came from above, not within. A great beam of energy shot up through the air and in a swirling gust of wind, they were gone.

The smug smile of triumph vanished from Ralston's face as he got to his feet again, having been knocked down by the force of Dawn's energy. "By the darkness!" he exclaimed. "What was that?" This was hardly a question the Creature could answer.

"It was a great rush of white energy," the Creature replied simply.

"Yes, you fool, I know *that*," Ralston retorted harshly. "Since when did Dawn acquire such immense power? Surely she cannot handle it? She will be at death's door with having used such magic. Weak and helpless," he mused. "She cannot use that energy again soon though, I think. And we still have one more of her companions to kill. He who would protect the Earth must die. Then, I shall unleash my complete darkness upon this unbalanced world."

And the Creature, for a moment, was afraid.

CHAPTER 18

The Breath of Life

C ASSANDRA SHIVERED AS THE wind blew through her auburn hair. She was just on the edge of Florian and had sat down upon the grass to rest. *Something has happened to Ian,* she thought restlessly. *If only I could do something more, but Madame told me to help the people. It was her last wish of me.* She sipped at a ceramic bowl of herbal tea she had made over a tiny fire.

At that moment, Cassandra heard the faint sound of grass being crushed underfoot. Without looking up, Cassandra said stoically, "What brings you to me, Kiara?"

Just as stoically, Kiara replied, "Fate, I suppose. I certainly didn't deliberately seek you out." *Chartreuse told me to talk to her, but I have nothing to say! I don't even know why I listened!*

"Have a seat," Cassandra offered quietly. "Would you like something to drink? I have only herbal infusions, but I am sure you can manage it."

Kiara merely stood in silence.

Looking up, Cassandra continued, "You have nothing to fear from me. I hold nothing against you."

Suddenly Kiara bristled. "What makes you think I would fear you? And I could care less if you hated or loved me. In my time, I was a trained warrior. I had skills you could only dream of!"

Taking a drink of tea, Cassandra paused. "That was a terribly long time ago. And it seems to me that when you died, you were in a luxurious castle apartment, a far cry from your warrior lifestyle."

Angrily Kiara spat back, "I gave it up for love, you fool! I was the best warrior Devona had, but I set it aside for Darius! Can you possibly understand that? I loved him so much that I sacrificed everything I had ever lived and worked for! No, I don't suppose you could understand." Kiara looked intently at Cassandra. "You are in love with Evan and yet you won't give up your priestess robes for him. What does that say about you, hmm? No answer, huh? You deserve to be alone," Kiara snapped. With that, she turned quickly and stormed away.

Cassandra sat for a moment and then suddenly threw her tea to the ground. There was the shimmer of a tear in her eye.

*   *   *

Though Florian was a beautiful meadow land of grasses, it gradually turned to stone as it gently sloped down to the sea. The group was now just on the outskirts of the capital city, Dale, which lay along the sea coast. Ian lay barely conscious on the ground, with his head in Mizu's lap. Evan was pacing about quickly, surveying their current location, while Dawn lay unconscious in Alan's arms with Robert close at hand.

"She's barely breathing!" Alan gritted angrily, staring down at Dawn.

"Yes, Alan, but she *is* breathing and we escaped Ralston for the moment," Evan pointed out, while he squinted against the setting sun. "Dawn knows what she is doing and she understands her limits. You must trust her. She will not allow herself to be taken down before her time." He turned back to the others. "How is Ian?"

Tearfully, Mizu replied, "He's having troubling taking in air. He needs help, Evan! Where is this Alethea he mentioned? Dawn asked the stone to take us right to her!"

"Darkness is coming soon," Evan sighed, massaging his temples. "And I don't mean evil. I mean the night. We need shelter."

"First we need to find Alethea!" Mizu cried passionately. Her hand was stained with Ian's blood, for she was holding the cloth on his wound.

"Won't someone here please start trusting in Dawn!" Evan cried out, this time angrily. There was something like fire in his voice. "She said she would take us to Alethea! Then she has! Can you not comprehend that?"

Everyone stared at the passion which had erupted from Evan. He was fairly glowing with fire. Then, came a voice, "What nice young people, coming to visit me all the way out here. I don't get many young visitors, especially at this hour. But don't mind me, I'm just rambling now. At my age, you are allowed to do that," she laughed.

Striding up over the hill was an old woman—but a remarkably fit old woman. Though she was skin and bone, she held her frame upright and there was a healthy glow of rose in the apples of cheeks. The woman's blue eyes sparkled with knowledge and her long gray hair was held back in a single braid, while a colourful rolled up bandana was tied around her head, holding back the strays. She wore a straight woolen dress dyed a medium blue. It was a practical dress to go with the practical boots upon her feet and practical black cloth bag over her shoulder.

"Alethea?" Evan asked, moving forward swiftly to meet her.

"Yes, indeed I am," she nodded, still smiling and then looked over at the others. "You and your friends need help. That one," she indicated towards Ian, "is grave."

"We have come here looking for your help. I believe you are the only one who can save him," Evan explained.

"Please help him!" Mizu cried.

Alethea's eyes narrowed with understanding. "Bring him this way. My home is near."

*   *   *

Evan and Robert carefully laid Ian down upon the bed in Alethea's little hut. The brightly painted white walls were made out of plaster, giving the place a sturdy feel. Dawn had been placed upon a makeshift bed of straw in one corner. There she rolled over and continued sleeping, unable to wake, due to sheer exhaustion.

Alethea came to kneel by Ian's bedside. She touched his forehead, gently lifting his soft blond locks. "He is burning with fever and he is scarcely taking in any air. One of his lungs is gone for sure." Her rosy cheeks quivered. "I can heal him, but the cost to me is very high."

"We have money . . ." Evan began, but Alethea shook her head.

"I was not referring to money from you. I said the *cost for me* is very high. Therefore, if I am going to pay it, I must know that it is worth it. Tell me quickly, why should I save this young man? Who is he? What is his purpose?"

Confused, Evan put forth, "He is Prince Ian, son of Prince Edric and Princess Carrie of Algernon. He is Queen Alice's nephew."

"That is what he was born into. Tell me again, *why should I save him*? Why does he matter?" Alethea looked desperately at Ian who was fading fast.

"He is the Guardian of the element Air. Only he can take the element into his soul and protect it from the grasp of the coming evil!" Evan pressed. *Can she possibly understand any of this?*

"It is an important role to be sure," Alethea nodded. "But you must understand how highly I have to pay. Please, tell me why he *matters*!"

Now Evan was becoming angry. "This is not a game! He is nearly dead!"

"Then why does he matter? You are missing the point," Alethea sighed in frustration. "You are missing the ultimate point of everything!"

"He matters because I love him! He matters to me!" Mizu suddenly broke from her reverie and stood up. "It is only Ian who can make waves inside my heart and awaken my emotion! Only he! He made me human! He made me a woman! He completes me! I *need* him! That is why he *matters*!"

"He is the best friend I ever had," Evan admitted suddenly. "He is like a little brother to me—always getting into trouble. He lacks discipline and fighting skills, but he can sing like no other. And he cares so deeply, even if he knows how things will end. Ian lives for the moment and is an example for us all. I am proud of him for that. He *is* my brother . . . I have no one else."

"He is a good friend," Alan put in slowly. "Useless in battle, but he is a good friend."

"With wisdom he doesn't even know he has," Robert agreed.

"And, my young friends, *that* is why he matters, thank you," Alethea nodded with tears in her kind bright eyes. "It is not our status, nor skills, nor destiny that makes us matter. It is what we mean to ourselves and others. Who do we matter to and more importantly, why do we matter to them. That is what is important. Now I know I can make the sacrifice without hesitation."

"Sacrifice?" Evan repeated uncertainly. "What are you talking about?"

Alethea looked at him softly. "I am going to save your friend's life. Did you think such magic could be utilized without enormous consequences? You know that all magic draws its strength from within us. I have the power to bring people back from the brink of death—not those already gone, but those at the dropping off point. Can you imagine what I must give?" She glanced down at Ian who was deathly pale and soaked in sweat and blood.

"When I bring someone back, it takes some of my own life energy away. Well, not just 'some'. Quite a lot actually. In my lifetime, I have saved only two others and I have become this old woman. I am only 17 years old, but I have given myself away to others who were worthy—not because I myself am unworthy, but simply because I have this gift to give. How many others, if they had this ability would use it? Hmmm? No one I'd wager. And that is why *I* matter."

Mizu came to stand before Alethea. "Please," she begged, "before it is too late. Save my Ian."

Alethea looked into Mizu's eyes and nodded. "I will." With that said, she gently leaned over the dying young man and kissed him softly on the lips. Though her body was old, the kiss she delivered was that of her true age. Mizu bristled at the sight. As Alethea kissed Ian, she held her palm lightly over his wound. When at last she parted from him, Alethea staggered backwards and collapsed to the ground. Evan rushed to her side and cradled her head. A dark shadow passed over his face as he looked up. "She is gone," he whispered. "Just as she said—only one more could be saved."

"She actually died, just like that?" Alan asked in disbelief. Though she had warned them, it was rather sudden. *We knew nothing about the poor woman . . . girl.*

"Magic, true magic, is serious business, which must never be taken lightly," Robert replied. "With magic we can do great things, but in turn, we must give great things. It is an exchange, not a gift."

"He's awake!" Mizu cried from Ian's side. She had not even turned around when Alethea fell. Her mind was completely upon Ian. Holding his hand tightly, she smiled as he opened his eyes. "You're alive," she whispered.

"Of course," Ian said softly and almost bitterly. "I *must* live." He felt his chest and took a deep breath of air. "That's better. Alethea . . . She was able to save me? I only remember her name in my fever."

"Alethea is gone, Ian," came Evan's voice from behind Mizu. "She sacrificed herself to save you."

"But why would she do such a thing for me, someone she has never even met?" wondered Ian as his eyes glistened.

"Because you matter to us," Mizu replied firmly. "And that is no small thing."

Ian pursed his lips and his brow knitted in uncharacteristic seriousness. *My life is not worth more than anyone else . . . I must not fail this brave woman. I must live and all will know her name. While I do not know her full story, I will at least pay tribute to her sacrifice.* "We must give her a proper burial," Ian whispered.

"There is no time," Evan responded quickly. "We will set a pyre aflame and continue on. The Web is unstable and I feel we must hurry and gather up the elements."

A scream broke through the air. Dawn was sitting up on the makeshift bed, staring at the body of Alethea. Her blue eyes were wide with shock and fright. "What is happening!" she cried.

Robert was the first one to Dawn's side. He placed a reassuring hand on her back and said solemnly, "Ian is alive."

*   *   *

The funeral pyre burned high, sending smoke billowing into the clear Florian air. It wasn't a proper or fitting pyre, but it was the best they could do in their hurry. Dawn leaned on Alan's shoulder, just as Mizu leaned on Ian.

A slight tear escaped the eye of Evan. *Truly, the world has lost a woman with a great heart. And in the end, there was no one but strangers to mourn her passing.* He clenched his fists and turned his back to the pyre. "We must go!" he shouted to the others. *We must keep moving.* He looked directly at Ian.

Ian's gaze hardened and he nodded. "It is time. The Air is very near."

CHAPTER 19

Meadow of Winds

WEARILY DAWN AND HER friends trudged down a well-worn path in the meadow country, Florian. It was a beautiful land to behold, with its vast greenness that did not seem affected by the season. Unfortunately, Dawn and her companions were far too tired and heartsick to notice much of the beauty. Dawn rode on Alan's back, as she had not yet recovered her full strength from having used the Eternal Diamond Rose. Still, there was a slight flush in her cheeks and Mizu, who had been watching Dawn from the corner of her eye, felt that the princess would make a full recovery. *She is strong, that one,* Mizu thought.

Ian's lips were pursed tightly as he marched alongside Mizu. *Paralda, I am coming! Where are you?*

A voice seemed to answer inside his head, *Look! Listen! See! Feel! The Air is around you!*

The group had just entered a rather large meadow which stretched beyond them some distance, before it gently sloped down into the calm blue ocean. Ian stopped with hearing this voice and stood still in the waving grasses.

"Ian? What's wrong?" asked Evan, placing a hand on his friend's shoulder. "Are you okay?"

Dawn hopped down from Alan's back with a serious expression. "He feels the power."

"This is it," Ian whispered, closing his eyes as a gentle breeze ruffled his hair. "The Meadow of Winds, we are here."

*   *   *

"How is he alive?" Ralston exclaimed in anger as he stared at Ian through a pool of Seeing Water. Ralston was currently situated just on the border of Florian. "I saw him die! What nonsense is this? Has the entire world gone mad?" He splashed the water with his hand, before standing straight and pacing about in frustration. "Senshi! Creature!" Ralston called his minions forward. "How hard is it to kill someone?" he asked with folded arms.

The Shadow Senshi looked at their feet and hesitated to answer. The Creature, however, did not. "Well now, that would depend on the person."

"Young people! Practically children!" Ralston cried out, his anger apparent.

"They are hardly children," the Creature pointed out. "But if you want them dead, perhaps you should be offering a better incentive."

Ralston raised his eyebrow, while the Senshi's ears perked up. Kage wondered what on earth this Creature of Magica's was hinting at. *Is he so obedient as he pretends? Frankly, I am afraid of that abomination. He is unpredictable, though Ralston thinks he has no will . . .*

"Anything is possible of course and anything can be done," the Creature went on, his eyes agleam. "You need only offer the right incentives. For instance, the Shadow Senshi here hate working for you and they hate you."

"Hey!" Kage exclaimed with a start. "Don't go putting words in our mouth!" *This is a dangerous game. Just what is he up to?*

"A soldier fights better, more intensely, when he is fighting for his own benefit. By forcing the Senshi to do your bidding simply because it is what you want, has caused them to work out of fear. Thus, they have held back their efforts and failed you. Frankly, they don't care whether you win or lose."

"What is your point?" Ralston gritted between his teeth as he stared hard at Kage who cringed.

"Give them incentive, my Lord," the Creature suggested. "Give them an offer and watch them fight for your cause. If they succeed, give them their freedom."

Kage swallowed hard and felt his entire body tense. Then, Ralston threw back his head and laughed. "Done!"

*   *   *

In this open field, I feel Paralda. I feel the soul of the Air. This is where things soar and fly. This is where ideas and creativity are born. This is the realm of boundless possibility.

The others watched as Ian stood some distance away from them in the sunny meadow. "Is this really the stronghold of Air? A Crystal Point?" asked Alan with some reserve. "It seems so plain compared to the Fire and Water. They were so elegant and grandiose."

"Things are never what they appear to be," Lord Robert spoke up. He had been rather quiet and pensive as of late. "Even the simplest of things may hold the greatest of power."

"You should have been a writer or a poet," Alan replied loosely, turning his attention to Dawn. "Hey what about that other stone your mother left?"

"It must be something of great power," Evan remarked, as Dawn fiddled with the collapsed version of the Light of the Earth around her neck.

"I honestly don't know what it does yet," Dawn admitted. "It seems different than the other stones . . . There is no particular energy coming off of it. Almost like . . . but that's impossible . . ."

"Dawn?" Evan pressed, sensing something odd in her voice.

Dawn hesitated before continuing, "Almost like it's a blank stone."

"How is that possible?" Alan wondered. "I thought all the Elf Stones were predetermined with the power of the Acjah."

"Well that's how I always understood it," Dawn replied. "I mean, it fit onto the torch, but it was as though it somehow did not belong."

"I am sure we shall find its purpose when the time comes," Evan nodded and then looked over at Ian.

Mizu had begun to approach Ian from behind, unable to contain her concern. "Ian," she began, only to be cut off by a tremendous gust of wind that threatened to sweep her off her feet.

Ian turned to face Mizu and the others. His face was a mixture of elation and concentration. "I am the AIR!" he declared, in a voice that seemed to carry across the land. "Always present, but always invisible. Always strong, but always unseen! You do not know me, but you know my works!"

Seemingly from nowhere, a great light began to radiate and illuminate the meadow with the colours yellow and white. Then, raining down like snowflakes, came hundreds of beautiful white feathers. They filled the air with a sweet perfume. Overhead, flocks of birds flew, forming patterns in the sky.

"You were saying something about this meadow being simple?" Robert commented to Alan, as the group stood together in awe.

Alan did not answer, but instead casually pulled Dawn closer to him. "Stay close, Dawn," he whispered. "Ralston could show up at any time."

"That's right," Evan nodded. "Ian needs to absorb this element quickly. We must not linger about."

"Is Mizu okay up there?" Dawn asked. "She is awfully close to that immense light. She's already on her knees . . ."

"Ian loves her and the Air knows that," Evan replied. "She will not be harmed."

Another huge gust of wind swirled around Ian and began to lift him off of the ground.

Ian's head swam and he blinked his eyes rapidly. Hovering before him was a man in white breeches with beautiful white feathered wings. He wore no tunic, so his wings extended freely out behind him. A yellow crystal dangled from a golden chain around his neck. "I am, Paralda, the Air and you, Ian, are my soul. We have been one for all eternity, whether you knew it or not. I am the song that emerges from your lips and I am the ideas that collect in your mind. We are the Air . . . We are life."

Ian nodded his head as he felt the truth in his heart. He said bravely, "Come to me and let us prepare for the revolution."

Paralda then moved forward, merging himself into Ian's form. Ian drew in a sharp breath of air and it was as though he were breathing for the very first time in his life. It was like being born again. And from Ian's back emerged two pure white wings. The wings moved up and down, causing the air about to swoosh down through the meadow.

Mizu was laying on the ground, knocked over by the force. As she slowly raised her head she saw Ian descending to the ground before her. "Those wings," she whispered in awe. The Water element inside her own soul recognized the being before her and she felt her own power respond.

As the light began to slowly fade, Ian reached out his hand to Mizu who did not hesitate to take it. As he raised her to her feet, Ian looked deeply into the Glintel's eyes. "I promise you, we shall always be together."

Mizu's eyes were wide, but she was not afraid. At this moment she knew in her heart that at some level, they would never be parted. The elements had bound them eternally, come what may in Fadreama.

In a bold move, Ian put his arm around Mizu's waist and drew her close to him. Using his white feathered wings, he enveloped them from the other's view. And suddenly, it began to rain.

CHAPTER 20

Moon Cycles

ASSANDRA STARED UP AT the shining moon. *Ah, Goddess, you grow bright with power. And then, when you begin to fade into darkness, so shall Fadreama. This is the last time I shall gaze upon your fully illuminated face.* At this thought, her heart hurt and her eyes glazed over. She stood amongst the marshes of Bainbridge, alone and feeling very tired. Cassandra had walked so far, in so short a time, putting down spots of evil that were cropping up everywhere. *It is an impossible task that I have been charged with. I am merely wasting my time until the end . . .* She looked up at the moon and clutched her chest. "In these end times, I wish only to spend my last days with Evan. Am I only to be granted a few last minutes? And I can't stop thinking about what Kiara said." This thought weighed heavily on her mind. *Nothing is fair!*

A floral scent blew by in the wind.

"I have been watching both you and Kiara," came Chartreuse's voice. "Between the two of you, I don't know who to root for." Her platinum hair gleamed in the moonlight as she approached Cassandra.

Humbly Cassandra looked down. "It does not really matter now, does it?"

"Do you think yourself nobler than Kiara, merely because you stick to your duty and deny yourself the last few pleasures of your existence?" Chartreuse asked boldly. "Is Kiara to be blamed for seeking out her own happiness? Is it so wrong for her to go after what she wants, honey?" Chartreuse spoke in all seriousness, but with a smile of understanding.

Cassandra processed this question for a moment. She had often thought Kiara selfish . . . but was she really? Was desiring happiness being selfish? "I do not think myself better than she," Cassandra replied evenly, keeping her voice calm. "I am only doing what I know—what I have been trained to do. You cannot blame me for that."

"And I don't," Chartreuse conceded, "but I *like* you Cassandra. You are faithful to Madame and have a good heart. Unfortunately, you are very stubborn. You know quite well that the end is nearing. For once in your life, do what you want! For the first and last time on this earth make *yourself* happy! Grasp at whatever tiny shred of happiness you can, before it is torn from you!" Chartreuse was now right before Cassandra and had a pleading look in her eyes. "It does not matter what anyone thinks or says!"

"Chartreuse . . ." Cassandra whispered.

"Take what you can and don't let it go. The world is ending, so what are you going to do? What is your top priority, honey? Now is the time to decide. Are you so stubbornly bound to duty that you would give up the last moments of happiness that you deserve and that . . . *he* deserves? Look at the torment Evan has endured for you!"

Cassandra started, for she had never thought of it in such a light. She stared at Chartreuse in wonderment.

"For all your knowledge and training, you cannot see it," Chartreuse sighed. "Evan has been bombarded by both Darius and Kiara, but he continually holds out for you, Cassandra. He holds out in the hopes that one day you may come to his side and stay there. Sure you may be there for the end, but that is the end. He needs to feel you now! He needs to know that his fight has been worthwhile! Your place, Cassandra, is obvious. It is at his side and nowhere else!"

"Always I have fulfilled my duty . . . but never the duty to my own heart. Perhaps I can learn a lesson from Kiara," Cassandra sighed. "Fadreama is lost and though I can keep working, nothing will change," she whispered. "My duty now is to . . . to Evan and myself—to nurture what we have, for as long as we can. Am I so weak and selfish?" she asked Chartreuse.

Chartreuse smiled and flipped her hair. "Madame would be proud of you."

* * *

"Alan, are you feeling quite alright?" Lord Robert asked the vampire who sat across from him at an outdoor table in one of Dale's charming little seaside cafes. The group had entered the city of Dale in order to take a brief rest before heading towards the neighbouring country of Bainbridge—and the final Crystal Point. They were battered, bruised, exhausted and fearful of what was to come.

Having taken a couple of rooms at a local inn, the group was now seated outside, enjoying the simple pleasure of drinks and sweets. This was something they never got to do anymore and they all knew it was their last opportunity to do it.

Alan was staring out at the glittering Beryl Ocean, absently watching the afternoon sunlight shimmer on the soft waves. The gentle climate and beautiful shoreline was something not found anywhere else in Fadreama. It seemed the epitome of culture and sophistication. The various carved statues and stone pillared temples were a testament to the artistic skill of the Florians.

"Alan?" Dawn repeated. "Robert is worried about you." She nudged Alan slightly and placed her hand on his wrist. Then thinking about the pain it may be causing him, she withdrew her hand, only to have him grasp it tightly.

"I was just thinking," Alan finally spoke in an unusually soft voice, "how beautiful this world truly is. I never appreciated it before. I guess I always took for granted that it would never end. I was so obsessed with my own family's problems that I never stopped to look beyond them." He sighed a little and his eyes were glassy. "There is so much we will not get to do."

Shocked by his sudden outpouring of emotion, Dawn said, "I think we were all wrapped up in our own little worlds. Maybe . . . maybe we were all a little bit selfish in our own way, but I think that is part of what it is to be human."

Suddenly Evan spoke up, "This may be the last time we can sit down together in a civilized manner." He cleared his throat and lifted his drink. "Therefore, I propose a toast."

Everyone lifted their glasses, waiting for Evan to continue. Dawn felt her heart tremble and she suddenly wanted to cry.

"A toast," Evan continued, "to this world and all the beautiful beings in it. A toast to those who lived and died protecting it. A toast to Queen Alice and King Alexander. Never did a country know such dedicated and great leaders. And a toast to Ian's parents, Prince Oliver and Princess Carrie. Their hard work on the land is an example to us all about what it is to persevere. A toast to . . ." Evan's voice cracked slightly, "A Toast to my mother, Princess Harmony, a woman of great strength and loyalty. To Queen Alexandria, an example of sophistication and regal enlightenment and to her daughter the most excellent Priestess Andrea. Not to mention brave Sienna, Princess of Stanbury. May she and her family rest in peace." He paused, thinking about his father. "And to Prince Andre." That was all he could think to say.

Sensing his momentum falter, Dawn picked up, "To Nissim, Octavius, Cloud Li, Kiraku, Sparks, Glimmer, Wisp, Madame Iris, Neva and other demons with good hearts, Ignatius and the rest of the Acjah—"

"Nalopa, Syoho, Queen L'eau and King Bleu," Mizu added with a nod.

"The Three Sisters," Ian put in.

"Boudicca, the Priestesses and the people of Hazelshire," Lord Robert spoke up.

"And to all those who came before us, like Captain Wyston and Barlow. We can't forget Emma, Clara and Priestess Lily. Not to mention Queen Rose Mary and King Alfred," Dawn added. "And to those souls looking for the light—Cousin Lance, Aunt Jewel, Dusk, and even . . . even Magica, Kane and Ralston."

"To Fadreama . . ." Alan whispered lifting his glass.

"To Fadreama."

They all drank with heavy hearts.

*   *   *

As night fell over the country of Florian, Alan restlessly paced his room at the Franceska Inn. The others had gone down to the hot spring baths owned by the inn. Florian was rich in natural hot springs, most of which were owned by inn and spa proprietors. The springs were rumoured to cure all manner of afflictions, while promoting good circulation and overall health. Believing it to be one of their last chances to recover their strength before the end, the others had gone down to the springs, leaving Alan, who had opted out. Dawn had been very concerned and perplexed by his behavior, but Alan had insisted that she go. "Go on and refresh yourself," he had said. "I'm going to stay at the room and lay down for a bit."

Laying down was the last thing on Alan's mind, though. The sun was now setting and the full moon rising. He could feel Syoho's cleansing power filling every part of his body. It tingled with a cool—not unpleasant—sensation. Alan gripped the stone window ledge and stared out at the ocean. The waves were a pale pink, as the sun was below the horizon. *This is a dangerous night for me, especially with my Crystal Point being next. What wretched timing!* He made a fist and brought it down hard upon the stone. "Ow!" Alan exclaimed, surprised by the pain this action elicited. "I am but a weak human, of no use to anyone."

A warm hand touched his shoulder—there was no pain and he had no batwings. "You are of great use and value to many, Alan."

He turned around to find Dawn. Her face held so much compassion, and honest love. Alan had never seen anything so raw, so pure, in his entire life. *Truly this woman is special among all others.* "I thought you were at the hot springs."

"I was," Dawn replied, "but I felt wretched leaving you alone. Then when I saw the moon, I knew I had to be by your side. You do not have to be alone."

"Your eyes . . . ," Alan said softly, ". . . . they are very beautiful. I don't think I've ever told you that, but I have always thought so, right from the moment I met you."

Dawn smiled. "Why, Shepherd Boy, I think you gave me a compliment. I just knew you had it in you. Perhaps the end of the world has something to do with it?" She gave a gentle laugh, as Alan suddenly pulled her close to him.

"I am sorry for my stubborn pride, Dawn."

Surprised, she replied, "We are all proud and stubborn to some degree."

He shook his head slowly. "My pride prevented us from having a real relationship, Dawn. Now we don't have much time left to enjoy this feeling. I never wanted to let myself feel it or admit it but . . . you have changed me, Dawn. In the darkest nights of my soul, you never lost your hope and faith."

Looking up into his face—*so handsome and kind* she thought—Dawn said, "I know you, Alan. I know your soul as clearly as though you had laid it bare before me." She paused, "I wish we weren't in this position. I wish we had more time. There are so many things I wish for, but they are things that perhaps we cannot be granted. I suppose we need to embrace what we have, while we can."

"It's not fair. There is so much I want to give you, Dawn."

"We don't live in a fair world. I do not think such a place exists, even in Syoho's land." *What my mother went through was not fair. What everyone went through was not fair. Perhaps that is the mystery of life—that we live, but nothing is fair. We always receive at a price.*

Gently Alan reached out and placed his hand upon Dawn's cheek. Then, in a fluid motion, they kissed and it was as though the world had stopped its evil, if only for a moment.

When they at last parted, Dawn whispered, "The others are not due back for at least another hour."

With a smile Alan replied, "Then let's enjoy like it's our last hour upon this earth." He kissed her again and the full moon glowed.

*   *   *

"I hope Alan is okay," Mizu said as the group made their way back up to their rooms from the hot springs. The inn rooms were located on the upper levels of the building, while the hot springs and spa occupied all the lower area.

"I'm sure Dawn is taking good care of him," Robert replied quietly. He had not said much the entire evening, preferring to keep his thoughts to himself. *I hope that at least Dawn is happy with her choice. But she must know that in the end, it can never be. It is too late for us all.* He sighed a little.

"Robert?" Evan put a reassuring hand on the man's back. "I hope you are okay with everything. Being blunt about it—I hope you are okay with Dawn and Alan."

"I won't lie to you and say that I'm fine," Robert replied. "But I have Dawn's happiness to think about. If she is happy, then let her do as she wishes, whether or not it is in her best interests. Though I may thoroughly disagree with her choice, it is beyond my control. Anyway, Nissim sent me to protect Dawn, not win her." *Though I sometimes wonder about that. What exactly did Nissim want from me? What could the old man see?*

"Nissim sent you?" Evan shook his head but continued, "Truly you must care for Dawn if you are to sacrifice your own happiness for hers."

"Soon, it will not matter anyway," Robert whispered and looked earnestly at Evan. "Only darkness now lies in our path, you know that, right? I am not trying to be morbid. It is a fact."

Pursing his lips Evan replied, "I like to think that in that darkness, we can shine a light. If Dawn is with us, then it will not be so dark. Believe in her, Robert. Believe that her destiny is greater than anything we could ever have imagined. I believe she is the one who can set everything straight. She can bring the elements and world back into balance."

"To do that, she may have to destroy us all." Robert looked uneasily up at the full moon and thought, *I shall never know happiness.*

CHAPTER 21

Shadow Senshi's Last Chance

"THANKS TO THAT CONNIVING Creature of Magica's, we now have *real* motivation to succeed," Kage told Itami and Kedamono, as they stood just outside the Francesca Inn in Florian. The full moon shone down brightly upon their figures, but Kage was not afraid of being caught. *These Florians are hardly security conscious. They care more about their art and music. See what good that does them!*

"If we succeed in killing the one called Alan, will Ralston truly set us free?" asked Itami suspiciously. Kedamono nodded his head in agreement with the question. "I mean, how far can we trust the word of Ralston Radburn? He is practically made of lies and deceit."

Kage folded his arms across his chest and nodded in agreement. "I have the same reservations, but there is really no other choice. It is obey or die. If he actually keeps his word, then so much the better!" Kage clenched his fists tightly and produced a phial of green liquid that glowed a ghastly hue. "This poison is a mixture of Catacomb Snake Venom and Devil's Spike Weed. Each element on its own is deadly, but to mix it together . . ." He began laughing.

"To be on the side of certainty, we ought to have Alan drink it all. Leave no room for escape," Itami declared with a nod.

Then, Kedamono flapped his arms wildly, causing Kage to nod. "You worry about his demonic vampire blood protecting him. No," he looked up at the full moon, "not tonight. Not tonight! The Creature has told us that on the night of the full moon, Alan reverts to his human form. He is completely vulnerable. He is ours to take down and take him down we shall. Dawn shall cry the tears of a thousand women very, very soon."

* * *

When Evan opened the door to the group's suite, he found Alan and Dawn leaning leisurely upon some over-sized cushions on a luxurious chaise lounge. Alan had his arm around Dawn's shoulders and her head was resting upon his chest. Clearing his throat so that the two heard him, Evan slowly opened the door wider for the others to enter.

Dawn looked up and smiled. "How were the hot springs? Sorry I bailed out at the last minute."

Mizu blinked her eyes a little in disbelief at the scene before her, but quickly recovered. "It was very refreshing, as water always is. I trust you are feeling rested? We have a long journey ahead of us tomorrow."

Dawn smiled and jumped up. "Yes, we will be ready tomorrow, won't we Alan?"

He nodded and swung his legs over the edge of the chaise lounge. "When the sun rises I will be a vampire again and my strength will return."

"That's right," Ian mused, "you are human with the full moon." He elbowed Alan lightly in the ribs. "Enjoying everything to the fullest, eh?"

"I . . ." Alan began, only to be quickly interrupted by Evan.

"Mizu is right. We have a difficult journey to Bainbridge tomorrow. We will use Dawn's eternal Diamond Rose, but we will take it in small steps, so as not to overtax her. Best get some rest, cousin," he smiled at Dawn, who was slightly flushed.

"Are you okay, Dawn?" asked Robert, finally getting up the courage to speak. *Oh Dawn . . . what have you done? Nothing about Alan is good for your future.*

"Yes, I'm fine," Dawn replied with a smile. "It's just a bit warm and humid in this country. I am hardly used to it. Algernon is really such a dry country."

"Quite so," Robert nodded as though he believed her words. His heart hurt very deeply, but he was determined to play the gentleman and serve Dawn as best he could. "Then I shall go fetch you a drink. It is the very least I can do," Robert attempted a smile.

Fooled by his feigned complacency, Dawn nodded cheerfully. "Yes, that would be lovely. We should all like something refreshing."

"Very well then," Robert agreed. "I will go down and bring back something spectacular."

"I'll come help you," Evan offered, only to have Robert tensely shake his head.

"No, no, Evan. You can stay up here and rest. I won't be long." With that, Robert made a swift exit out the door. An awkward silence then hung in the room.

Ian cleared his throat and said, "I really wish I could have visited this country sooner. Truly it is my type of lifestyle!"

"I'm sure those ladies at the hot springs had nothing to do with it," Mizu laughed sarcastically.

"What ladies?" Ian asked with a smile. "You were the only lady I saw."

At this, Mizu laughed. "Oh come off it!" She shook her head, but her eyes looked adoringly at Ian. She was not angry at all.

*   *   *

"Our mode of action approaches," Kage whispered to Itami and Kedamono. The demons had taken over the inn's kitchen. About a dozen or so of the inn's staff lay dead on the ground, done in by Kage's malice. "He is coming to order. Give him these drinks, no matter what he orders," Kage said to the one remaining servant, who trembled in fear. Kage held out a tray with six goblets on it. Each goblet had a name engraved upon it. Holding the phial of glowing green poison, Kage emptied it completely into the goblet with Alan's name upon it. The poison dissolved in an instant and looked like just another glass of exotic fruit juice with a hint of liquor.

"Maybe we should have poisoned all the goblets," Itami wondered nervously.

"Forget it!" Kage snapped. "I'm not taking any chances! All the poison is in Alan's cup. It's enough to take down a giant. He will perish for sure!"

The waiter took the tray with trembling hands and Kage directed him to the door. In a whispered voice Kage said, "Smile and remember, compliments of the house."

*   *   *

Robert had a frown upon his face. *How can Dawn set her heart upon Alan? Just look at all the pain he has caused her! He has been rude beyond belief—deliberately! Can he honestly think to care for her and love her like I can? Is he truly capable of such love after his trauma? Sometimes I wish . . . no, I should never wish such things—not in our position.*

Looking up, Robert gave a servant a weak smile. "Drinks please. Six of them. Is there something refreshing you recommend?"

The servant held out a tray in a mechanical fashion. "Compliments of the house." He then walked away, knowing full well it was to his death.

Robert took the tray with a confused look. *That servant was so pale, as though he were heading towards the gallows.*

*   *   *

"Our names are engraved on the goblets!" Dawn exclaimed as she held the crystal in her hands. "Are we meant to keep them afterwards?"

Robert shrugged. "The server didn't say. He just handed me the tray and said 'compliments of the house'."

"Hospitality all around," Ian sighed in contentment. "Mizu, we should stay here and live out the rest of our lives together."

Mizu laughed and playfully punched him in the shoulder. "What, are you suggesting we should get married?"

"I suppose it's the honourable thing to do, after all," Ian smiled and tipped his goblet back.

"To honourable intentions—however misguided they may be," Mizu laughed, taking a drink.

"There is not much honour left in the world," Alan said quietly, looking at his drink.

Softly Dawn touched his back. "If you maintain honour in your own heart, then it does not matter what others are doing."

Alan smiled, a true and genuine smile. "The world needs more people like you, Dawn." He then placed the goblet to his lips and drank heartily, only to collapse a mere second later.

Dawn jumped up screaming, for there was no mistaking that Alan was dead before he had hit the ground.

CHAPTER 22

Dawn's Sacrifice

DAWN WAS IN ABSOLUTE hysterics—something she had never succumbed to before. "Please, calm down," Mizu held Dawn by the shoulders, as she sat the screaming girl down in a chair. Mizu knew only too well what Dawn was feeling. *And there is no Alethea this time to help us . . .*

"NO NO NO! It cannot be real! It cannot be happening!" Dawn cried. She put a hand to her stomach and shook hard with her sobbing. At this moment she could not slow her mind down long enough to consider any course of action.

"Dawn!" Mizu exclaimed, adding a firmness to her voice that she rarely, if ever, used. "Dawn, look at me!"

The authority in her voice seemed to reach Dawn, even in her agitated state, for the girl managed to connect her eyes with Mizu's. Gripping Dawn's hand, Mizu continued, "We are in danger right now. We cannot stay here. Ralson and his minions will be coming soon to see if the job is done. We *must* not be here when they arrive, do you understand?"

"But it is all over!" Dawn cried. Her blue eyes were so pained, they could have broken the heart of even Ralston himself. "Don't you see? Without Alan, without the Earth, we cannot do what we were charged to do! The Earth cannot be protected without Alan!"

Mizu pursed her lips tightly, for she knew that Dawn spoke the truth. Then, Evan piped up. He had been leaning over Alan's rigid form on the bed in anguish. "We must not think of that now. Our thoughts must be on our own preservation. We cannot think of a solution if we too are gone."

"Yes, Dawn, we must flee quickly," Robert added. "We can collect our thoughts far from here."

Only Ian remained out of the conversation.

Dawn stood up angrily. "NO!" she cried out firmly. "No! I will not leave him. I will not run away to save myself!"

"But Dawn, Alan is gone," Robert pressed gently.

"I was gone too," Ian spoke up softly. "I was dead, but I could still see and hear what was happening . . . The silver cord was not yet severed. If you had all decided that it was over for me, I would have passed into the light. But you did not leave me and you did not give up. So I now stand here before you, though at a great cost. There must be a price for Alan's life. I know that he has not yet passed into the light. He has too much business left here in Fadreama. If we act quickly, he may yet be preserved. And no, I do not know how."

Mizu was at a loss for words. *It's true. I would never have given up on Ian. How could I possibly expect Dawn to do the very thing I could not?*

"Alethea is gone though," Robert pointed out. "Who can bring him back?"

"One who is willing to pay a price," Evan replied looking at Dawn. "Cousin, you are the only one among us who may be able to do something, but be warned, what you may give—" She interrupted him.

"I don't care," Dawn replied, wiping away her tears and bringing forth the Light of the Earth in a brilliant flash. "I am always changing my destiny. The Three Sister's predicted I would kill the one I love. I will NOT. I will defy their words. I will *save* him." Before anyone could react she shouted, "TIME!" With this exclamation, the Time Stone flared up and stopped everything, everywhere. Only Dawn was now able to move. Sweating with the effort, she weaved around her frozen companions and looked at Alan's lifeless form on the bed. "You are still here," she whispered. "Wait for me. In the end, we shall go into the light together. You cannot leave me alone."

Dawn hardly knew what she was doing as she stepped into the center of the room, held her hands aloft and closed her eyes, entering into a deep meditative state. *Ignatius,* she whispered in her mind. *Ignatius of the elves. I have need of you and the Acjah. We must make a bargain and we must make it now. You know the situation. Please . . .*

In her mind, Dawn was now standing back in the shining garden of Etain. It was as lovely and unchanged as ever. Ageless, beautiful and stagnant was the land of the elves. And there stood Ignatius, along with King Sunel and Queen Starel along the jeweled main street. Their forms stood tall, slender, ethereal—grace was second nature. Their aura's glowed white and though they sparkled, their faces were solemn indeed.

"Princess Dawn," Ignatius greeted her. "We meet one last time, at the end of all things." His face was sad, for Dawn was like an adopted daughter to him and he knew that she was going to make a grave decision.

"You know why I have called you," Dawn replied, feeling the strain of the Time Stone. "I seek to change what cannot be changed. I seek to undo that which is done. I seek life from death."

"You understand that such a thing has a high price?" Queen Starel spoke up. Her voice flowed over Dawn like the gentle trickling of water.

"Anything," came the Princess's firm reply. "I love Alan. There isn't anything I wouldn't do for him."

"The Three Sisters predicted you would kill him," King Sunel pointed out. "Should you bring him back, you may still cause such harm to come to him."

"It is not yet time for Alan to go," Dawn replied firmly. "And when *we* do go, it will be on our own terms." Her face was set in a determined expression and her fists were clenched tightly.

Ignatius sighed and looked at the King and Queen, before looking back at Dawn. "This is a one time favour and once done, we can provide you with nothing else ever again. By doing this, we risk angering the powers that be."

"We are at the end anyway," Dawn replied quietly. "Please."

Queen Starel came forward and, leaning towards Dawn, said, "We shall give Alan back the breath of life this one time. But in return, you must surrender the Light of the Earth back to Ignatius, along with all the stones, save the two that your mother gave you. Those were not true Elf Stones, but merely magical stones that were compatible with our magic."

"This means you will no long be able to contact the Acjah or use our key—that must be returned as well," King Sunel added. "All ties to the Acjah and yourself will be cut. No longer an Elf Friend shall you be." *But,* Ignatius thought to himself, *always a friend to me.*

"Of course, you may have it back," Dawn nodded quickly. *I will have no more magical powers. I will be facing Ralston without the aid of the Light and must rely on my own spirit. So be it, for Alan's sake. I will not let him down.*

"There is more," Ignatius said quietly. "And this runs much deeper. Dawn, you must give up 16 years of your own life span—one year for each we are returning to Alan. However long you would have lived will be shortened by that amount."

"Done." Dawn's face was set in a hard, unemotional line. "You could have taken 50 if that was what you needed. I love him. And I know he would do the same for me. Love has no bounds. Take it.

Take it all. Just give me back Alan." There were no tears in her eyes, no indication that she grieved for what she was giving.

"It has been an honour to know you, young Dawn," Ignatius bowed. "You have shown us, yet again, how courageous and good humans have the ability to be." He glanced sideways at the King and Queen who pretended not to notice. Then, from the door in one of the tree homes, emerged Lavena, Ignatius's daughter and Nissim's twin sister. She was carrying a box—for the Light of the Earth.

Lavena approached Dawn and opened the box. "If you please, Princess Dawn." Lavena's eyes were soulful and expressive, an indication of her half-human heritage. "Do not think you are losing, Dawn," she whispered. "You have love and that is better than any amount of power or magic. It is something not everyone is blessed with."

Without hesitation, Dawn placed the torch into the case and it was snapped shut. All the work she had put into acquiring Elf Stones was gone. She had given it all up.

"And now, you must return to the waking world, for you are no longer in possession of the Time Stone," Ignatius said quickly and the natural flow has returned. "You will not be drained from having used the stone as you normally would. That is my last gift to you. Awaken and reap what you have sown. So be it."

In a flash, Dawn opened her eyes and found herself standing in the bedroom of the Francesca Inn. Her friends were all staring at her expectantly, when suddenly a voice said, "Dawn."

Alan stood by the bedside, looking untouched by death which had not so long ago taken him. Dawn rushed into his arms, leaving her confused friends gaping.

"Why did you give that for me?" Alan whispered into her hair. "Your magic—your life. Dawn . . ."

"You would have done the same for me, Alan," she said softly. "I could not bear the thought of going on without you. It was just wrong. I love you too much for my own good."

"And I am tied to you forever, Dawn, even if the world falls into the abyss. I will always find you again." In a softer breath he said, "I love you more than you can ever know."

In their own world they kissed, only to have Evan clear his throat and say, "I have no idea what just happened here," his eyes were shining with emotion, "but we can discuss it later. Right now, we need to leave. I feel the web shaking. Ralston is slithering his way here and we must flee to Bainbridge before he realizes a miracle has taken place."

Dawn produced the stone her mother had given her—the Rose Stone. She held it in her hands softly. "Not a miracle . . ." she whispered.

"Dawn, where is the Light of the Earth?" Mizu asked.

"I gave it back," she replied softly and the Eternal Diamond Rose glowed brightly in her hand, as they all disappeared from the room.

CHAPTER 23

In the Marshland

WHEREAS FLORIAN WAS A bright coastal hub of activity and fine arts, Bainbridge was just the opposite. It was a dimly lit and drab looking country, shielded by a thin film of clouds that would never break. The land was dangerous with bogs and sinkholes, making travel across it perilous. Thankfully the early inhabitants of Bainbridge had built a series of pathways across the country, though this meant that you could not always choose your route—it had been chosen for you long ago and if you should be so silly as to forge your own path, your only destination would be under the marshland, in its death grip. Many a poor soul had vanished beneath the bog in either desperation or stupidity.

"How come everyone else got the attractive countries?" asked Alan as he eyed Bainbridge from the outskirts. His lip twitched at the gloomy scene before him. He was now a vampire again and his bat wings flowed out behind him.

"Well now, whether or not something is attractive, depends entirely upon one's own point of view," Robert commented in a voice which suggested a deeper meaning lay beneath his words.

"The Crystal Point will either be in or near the capital city of Cerridwen," Evan mused. ""What does your heart tell you, Alan?"

After a pause, Alan shook his head slowly. "My heart tells me that after this, everything will soon be over."

"Now none of that," Ian piped up, hands on his hips. "Cerridwen, eh? That is another name for the great Goddess—The Lady. It is said that Cerridwen is the ultimate representation of the Goddess and of women. She represents all three aspects of the Goddess—the young maiden, the caring mother and the wise crone. And yet legend says that it is for the crone aspect that Cerridwen is the most known. They report she has a cauldron of wisdom called the Cauldron of Earth, through which anything can be seen and known."

"Thank you for that lesson," Mizu laughed slightly. "But come on now, we must travel as far as we can on foot, to spare Dawn the agony of transporting us." The Princess was currently sitting quietly on a boulder by the roadside—possibly the last boulder between there and Cerridwen.

Lifting her head, Dawn smiled lightly. "Cerridwen's Cauldron also brings about birth, rebirth and transformation. That is certainly comforting, don't you think?" She stood with great effort. "I do not believe in endings. I only believe in beginnings. Now let's start moving."

Alan gave Dawn a smile and offered his arm.

*   *   *

"How could you have failed?" Ralston roared at the Shadow Senshi. "He drank the poison! He was dead! His soul had passed on! How is this possible?"

Kage shifted uncomfortably. *This is not our fault!* "The Princess," he replied quickly.

Ralston narrowed his eyes. "That wretched girl! Always she is foiling my plans!"

"But hear this," the Creature spoke up. "Dawn brought Alan back at a great cost—part of her life and all of her Elf magic."

"You don't say . . ." Ralston mused, his eyes gleaming. "So in a battle, Dawn may be a little less intimidating." He paced about the inn room in Florian, while massaging his temples. "Surely they are already into Bainbridge—wretched place! I despise going there myself. Not only is it dangerous, it is downright creepy! Yes, even *I* say that! The people in that land are wild, savage, untouchables. They are indeed the most primitive people in all of Fadreama and yet have a most dangerous army. Will Dawn and her cohorts even make it to the Circle of Stones where the Crystal Point lies?" Suddenly Ralston laughed evilly. "Surely they will be torn to pieces by the Bainbridge people before they get very far. Perhaps we ought to just wait and see . . ."

Kage held his tongue. *Wait and see! The demon simply doesn't know what to do! Dawn foils him at every turn! If we can destroy Dawn now, surely Ralston will free us. He is not sending us this time because he does not want us to succeed and be free. Well! We shall see who is more clever! Dawn herself will die by my hand.*

And so, when Ralston had his attention focused elsewhere, the Shadow Senshi secretly departed for Bainbridge.

"Where have the Senshi gone to in such a hurry?" the Creature asked Ralston.

An evil smile crossed Ralston's face. "They have gone to Bainbridge to kill Dawn."

"You did not send them?"

"No, Kage took it upon himself. He hopes to be free and so has motivation to try a little harder," Ralston explained calmly.

"You will help them? Bainbridge is an unstable place."

"I will not lift a finger for them," Ralston replied. "If they fail in this, then it is the last time. I have less and less need for such baggage."

The Creature shuddered.

*   *   *

"Why do you think the sky is so dark here?" Dawn wondered as she made her way carefully along the elevated stone path through the dangerous Bainbridge marshes. A mosquito buzzed noisily by her ear.

"They say that when the realms were separated, something happened to Bainbridge. They were connected to the fairy realm and when they parted, Bainbridge fell into depression," Ian piped up. "It was something of a traumatic loss, I gather."

"I suppose it makes sense," Dawn mused. "Alexandria would be a difficult place to get cut off from. It is truly a powerful kingdom— ow!" she cried, holding her hand to her neck. A little black pebble bounced to the ground. "How strange . . ." Dawn bent down to pick it up, just a shower of black pebbles fell from the sky like raindrops.

"Look out!" Alan and Robert both cried, scrambling to shield Dawn. They gave each other a defensive look and Robert backed off, while drawing his white bow.

"Where is it coming from?" Mizu exclaimed, covering her head with her hands. The tiny black pebbles continued to rain down upon them, inflicting numerous bruises.

"The sky!" Evan cried. "Look to the sky!" High above them, against the grey backdrop of clouds, were tiny dark figures riding upon what looked to be . . .

"Pegasus-Unicorns!" Dawn shouted in amazement. "Just like my mother's friend, Wisp! Those are the same as Wisp!"

"But what of the people riding upon them?" Robert wondered. "I hesitate to shoot at those who may simply be misunderstanding us."

"If they are . . . or were . . . friends of Alexandria, then surely they must bow to a descendent of that realm," Dawn mused, though no one else heard her.

The attackers swooped in lower and began yelling something in a foreign language. It was a tongue that no one in the group had heard before. There was a primitiveness to it that was all at once fierce and yet childlike. The people who rode upon the Pegasus-Unicorns appeared quite small in stature and were dressed in various animal skins. Their hair—both the men and the warrior-like women—was wild and dark, with a few stray braids swinging in the wind. Blue and black face paint adorned the warriors in stripes across their bare arms, ankles and cheekbones. Truly they were a sight to behold—ferocity in its most pure form, untainted by hate. They were defending their land from invaders, nothing else.

"We cannot fight them!" Evan exclaimed while shielding his head from the falling stones. "They are not the enemy!"

"But how do we reason with them?" Robert wondered. "They do not understand our words and just getting their attention seems absurdly difficult!"

"If they but knew there was Alexandrian blood down here, they might think differently," Dawn put forward with a nod to Evan. "They mourn the loss of Alexandria . . . we both have such blood!" Without thinking, she released her fairy wings.

As the Bainbridge warriors swooped in lower, their Pegasus-Unicorns let out the most heart wrenching wail.

"Please!" Dawn cried. "Please! We are not here to hurt you!" Alan shielded her from an onslaught of stones.

"As if they understand reason," he muttered.

Then, like a voice from beyond, sounded the words, "Adixovi devina devada andagin vindiorix cvam vnai!" These words clearly resounded through the air like a ringing bell, stopping the warriors mid-attack.

Evan spun around at the sound of the voice and stared in wonderment. "Cassandra!"

With a smile that was truly heartfelt, Cassandra strode forward, her priestess gowns flowing gently in the moss-scented breeze. She looked like a beautiful apparition, floating across the deserted marshland. And to one man, she was the entire world. Stopping in front of Evan, Cassandra continued to smile. "I am by your side to the end. No more fighting alone. No more wandering. My place is right here. It took me some time to find it, but I suppose there is a reason for that too."

Evan's eyes were glistening and he could utter no words to describe his complete joy. "There is some happiness yet to be had in this weary world," he whispered.

The strange and fierce Bainbridge tribes lowered themselves almost to the ground and stared suspiciously at the group. Their

Pegasus-Unicorns did not have the same suspicious eyes, but were instead neutral and calm looking. Their large expressive eyes looked on with curiosity and a deeper wisdom. The one warrior who looked to be the leader, actually allowed his Pegasus-Unicorn to land upon the pathway. He was small, with very white skin, black hair and intense piercing black eyes. His long dark hair had random tiny braids, which had then been half gathered up at the back of his head and bound with a leather string. As he suspiciously surveyed the group, his eyes landed upon Evan and Dawn. His eyes opened wide and he gave a great shout to those hovering in the air behind him. Ripples of whispered rang through the air.

Cassandra looked on with satisfaction. "As I thought," she said, "they have finally realized that there is fairy blood among us. We are now allies. The fairies of Alexandria are like the Lord and Lady to them."

"They must take us to where the Earth Spirit resides," Dawn told Cassandra breathlessly. "My ability to fight is gone, so we must not linger."

Cassandra gave Dawn a tender look. "Do not think, my dearest princess, that you are without power. The Elf Magic was never truly yours to begin with." Cassandra then turned to the Bainbridge tribesman—specifically the little man with intense eyes. She uttered a string of foreign phrases to the man, who nodded in agreement.

"The Web," Evan spoke up urgently, "it is shaking with great anger. I think it is the Shadow Senshi!"

The little man was summoning several riders from the sky. They each lowered themselves to the ground and the Pegasus-Unicorns gently bent their knees to lower themselves further.

"We must ride with them," Cassandra explained. "They know where we must go."

"I can fly myself," Alan said a little crossly. "And I can carry Dawn with me."

"You underestimate the speed with which the Pegasus-Unicorns fly," Cassandra said a little tightly. "Now get on, we have to move quickly!"

Alan eyed the little men suspiciously.

"Please, Alan," Dawn said, "just do it."

With a little huff, Alan strode up to one of the bowed Pegasus-Unicorns and heaved himself up on top, behind one of the men. The little man neither flinched nor made any sign of emotion regarding his passenger. However, a strange look of horror briefly passed over Alan's features and then was gone.

Ian, Cassandra and Mizu were next to mount the magnificent creatures. When Evan approached one of the horsemen, a look of reverence appeared on the man's face. He gave a little bow as Evan climbed aboard and had the look of one who has been given a great honour.

However, it was Dawn herself who caused quite a stir among the little dark-eyed men. She came up to the only remaining horseman—the leader. His piercing eyes locked on hers and Dawn felt as though he could see exactly who she was. *He has the eyes of one who can truly see . . .* she thought. The man extended his hand to her and she gripped it tightly as he helped her onto the warm back of the Pegasus-Unicorn. Dawn had rode Wisp many times, though never bareback. It was certainly a different feeling. Uncertainly, Dawn held onto the waist of the Bainbridge leader, fascinated by the myriad of blue tattoos covering his back and arms. She held her breath as they ascended and only out of the corner of her eye, noticed the look of fear on Alan's face. He was not, however, looking at her.

Alan clenched his fists hard and felt sweat trickle down his brow. *The Earth . . . she is screaming . . . screaming . . .*

CHAPTER 24

One Last Time

*I*T WAS HOURS BEFORE the legion of Pegasus-Unicorns and their riders descended upon the city of Cerridwen—if one could call it a city at all. By most standards, it was something more akin to a large village with many individual thatched huts surrounding one very large mead hall. This settlement was surrounded on all sides by marshland so that it floated like an island in the midst of an ocean of bog. Behind the hall, only a short distance away, was an open area with a circle of large stones.

As the Pegasus-Unicorns landed and all dismounted, Dawn rubbed her burning eyes and licked her dry lips. She was so very exhausted and the expressions upon her companions' faces indicated that they were as well. *And yet there is little time for rest,* Dawn thought wearily. *Not yet anyway.*

Dawn and her companions were instantly surrounded by the Bainbridge villagers—including children dressed in animal skins. They were all staring in wonder at Dawn and Evan.

"They see your fairy wings," Cassandra explained softly. "You are very much like deities to them. They believe you have come here because it is the end. They believe," she paused as a lump formed in her throat, "that you bring death."

Looking out at all the expectant faces, Dawn felt her chest tighten. "Tell them we bring transformation."

As Cassandra spoke, Mizu gripped Ian's arm tensely and said, "Do you feel your element stirring impatiently within you? The energy . . ." she placed a hand to her forehead, "is waiting to explode . . ."

Patting her hand reassuringly, Ian said, "Trust that Dawn will set everything right soon."

Cassandra delivered Dawn's words to the people and the man who had carried Dawn spoke up. Cassandra nodded and said, "This man is called Bran and he is the chief or king of Bainbridge. He says he is at your service, even though you bring death."

Dawn sighed. "Cassandra, we need to take whatever rest we can get. Though I doubt it will be much, can Bran provide us with some place to gather our strength?"

As Cassandra was delivering this request, Alan suddenly lurched forward gripping his head. In a cold sweat, he fell to the ground.

"Alan!" Dawn was at his side, cradling his head.

"Earth," Alan whispered before losing consciousness.

"Cousin," Evan said to Dawn, "I think Alan was overpowered by the screams of the Earth. He may need to rest before we head onward to the Crystal Point. I know there is little time, but . . . he is of no use to the Earth in this condition." Evan shrugged and rubbed his weary eyes.

"Bran will provide us with accommodations," Cassandra announced with a nod. "When you feel ready, he will take you to the Crystal Point."

Chief Bran ordered some of his people to show Dawn and the others to their lodgings. A couple of the small, but strong, little men hoisted up Alan and carried him away with ease. Evan and Cassandra held back a bit and walked behind the others.

"This will be a short rest," Evan sighed.

Cassandra placed her hand on his arm. "I am glad to take that rest with you, however short."

Looking into her eyes, Evan smiled lightly. "Me too."

"I . . . spoke to Kiara not so long ago," Cassandra admitted suddenly. "She sought me out, it seems. Whatever she came for she changed her mind about. She is hurting so deeply . . ."

"I know," Evan said softly. "I wish there was something I could do to put her soul to rest before the end. She should never have been brought back. She should never have had to relive the pain of the past. It is cruel."

"I suppose that's why we forget when we are reborn," Cassandra agreed. "Each lifetime has its own sorrows . . . we needn't be burdened with those that came before."

Evan could only sigh again.

*   *   *

Kiara stood uncertainly outside of the hut where Evan and the others were resting. She spoke the language of the Bainbridge villagers, but that had not mattered since none had detected her presence. Kiara could be as skillful as a priestess when need be.

Why am I even here? Chartreuse told me to come, but now that I'm here, I hardly know what to say. And Cassandra is here too . . .

A heavy wind blew by, laden with the musty smell of the bog. It was a silent and lonely place. Kiara thought it was very much like a ghost land. *This is pointless . . .* Just as she turned to go, the light of a torch illuminated the ground. Turning around, she saw Evan standing before her. Though Kiara was rarely surprised, she started a little.

"Evan . . ." she murmured his name softly.

"Kiara," he said coming forward, "we need to settle this. There is very little time left." He reached out and took her hand. "I have a gift for you." He bowed his head and fell silent.

Back at the hut, Cassandra looked on with worry. *Evan, I hope you know what you are doing . . .*

"A gift?" Kiara asked. "What are you talking about?"

Then Evan raised his head slowly and it took a moment for his eyes to focus. In a voice that was not his own, he said, "Kiara."

Kiara bristled and her heart nearly jumped out of her chest. "Daris," she whispered, eyes glistening.

In an instant, Darius had his arms around Kiara. It was an embrace that had waited thousands of years to happen. "I never thought I would speak to you again," he whispered. "You do not know what torment it was to see you, but not be able to do anything. Evan is very strong. His will held me at bay."

"You broke free then?" Kiara asked with hope in her voice and tears in her eyes.

Darius paused. "My love . . . Evan *allowed* me this chance . . . to say goodbye."

"Goodbye?" Kiara was in shock. "But, my dearest! You are free now! We can be together!"

Stroking her pale hair, Darius shook his head. "Kiara, the world is ending. The goddess Syoho has left us. And Evan has one last duty to perform. Only now do I realize that our time . . . came and went, long ago."

"No!" Kiara began to sob into his chest. "No! Not again! Not again! I will not lose you again!"

Darius seemed to be fighting his own emotions. "Kiara, I am so sorry for failing you in the past. I died . . . I could not protect you. I fell into a trap when I should have known better. I should have just married you and not cared what anyone said."

"It was my fault!" Kiara exclaimed passionately. "I was tricked by Ralston! *I* should have known! I was trained but I did not see! I am so sorry! You died because of me!" Thousands of years of regret came pouring out.

Taking Kiara firmly by the shoulders Darius said, "No, Kiara. I did not die because of you. I died because of Ralston. You died because of Ralston. All these years my soul blamed itself. All these years your soul blamed itself. We could not find peace . . . but now, now we can, because Evan and his friends have the best chance of defeating Ralston Radburn."

"But, Darius! I love you! I want to be with you!" Kiara exclaimed passionately. Her tears had stained Evan's tunic and continued to flow freely.

"Oh, Kiara," Darius said pulling her close. "I love you too, more than I think you ever realized in life. And I will go on loving you for all eternity. No matter how many times I am reborn, some part of that soul will forever be devoted to you. But . . . we could only be Daris and Kiara once. Despite the pain . . . I am grateful for that."

Kiara was silent for a moment. Out of the corner of her eye she had spied Cassandra waiting by the door of the hut. Blinking back the onslaught of tears, Kiara lifted her head to look at Darius. "No matter who I become or who you become, some part of me shall always love you, Darius. And someday . . . our souls shall meet again and we will remember our love at the same time. Someday, we will have our time together and maybe . . . maybe then, things will have a happier ending."

With that said, they kissed. And when at last they parted, Kiara said, "Cassandra, send Dawn out here."

Startled, Cassandra complied. Within moments, Dawn was running outside and immediately realized what was happening.

Kiara held up her hand to stop Dawn from speaking. "Please, Your Highness, remove the Fragment of Cardew that was forced upon me."

"Kiara, I—" Dawn began but was interrupted.

"Yes, I know what will happen and I welcome it. When I died I saw the most beautiful welcoming light. But I was so angry that I turned away from it. Now I see it again and I want to enter it."

Dawn nodded and placed her hand on Kiara's forehead.

"Cassandra," Kiara said to the priestess who stood behind Dawn, "treasure it while you can."

Cassandra swallowed hard and nodded. "Thank you."

Dawn's hand began to glow along with Kiara's entire body. It only took a moment and when the light faded, Kiara was gone. Yet Dawn could see within her mind's eye, the most lovely door of light. Kiara stood before it and all the grief she possessed in life was gone.

Her face seemed a thousand times lighter. She gave a small smile before walking through the door.

Dawn now turned her attention back to Evan. He blinked twice and quietly said, "Cassandra."

CHAPTER 25

Cerridwen's Cauldron

A GREAT CRY OF TORMENT from inside the hut shook the night. Dawn's eyes widened as she exclaimed, "Alan!"

Root deep in the Earth,
But don't spread like the weed.
For in grasping too much,
You shall be consumed only by greed.

Alan came staggering out of the hut holding his head. "The Earth . . ." he managed to say between gritted teeth, "she is screaming . . . I need to free her . . . Please, Dawn!" He looked up and his eyes were wide and pained.

Nodding quickly, she turned to Cassandra, "You must order the chief to take us to the Crystal Point now! Alan's impatience must mean darkness is on the move again!"

Alan's cries had roused Bran, his warriors and many of the people. They now made their way towards the group, just as Robert, Ian and Mizu emerged from the hut looking weary. Bran went immediately to Cassandra and rattled something off rapidly in his language. He indicated towards the sky, obviously agitated.

Looking up, Cassandra whispered, "No . . . The Shadow Senshi!"

"By the Power," Evan breathed, "there is such a black aura of malevolence about them! They are so angry! The hate is shaking the Web like an earthquake! I have never felt such an energy about them before! This may very well be them or us this time!" *And it had better be us!* Pulling out his sword, Evan struck a barrier, holding its glittering form in the air about them. "Take Alan to the Crystal Point!"

Cassandra spoke swiftly to Bran, who had already drawn a sword of his own and several others had bows ready. After replying to Cassandra, Bran came to stand beside Evan. He nodded and it did not take words to solidify their alliance. His warriors followed suit, including the women, while any children were guided away by the elderly.

"The Circle of Stones is behind the great mead hall. The Crystal Point is within them," Cassandra said. "You must run! This lady will show you the way!" She pointed to a young lady in an uncharacteristically long leather tunic. Her hair was fastened into several braids, with bog grasses woven into them. The mysterious blue markings on her face seemed to give her the aura of authority.

"Cassandra, what of you?" Dawn asked in a panic, as the Bainbridge woman made motions for them to follow.

"I will stay here to fight with Evan," Cassandra replied firmly. "He needs my power. The rest of you must go, now! You will have no further need for translations! That is Bran's daughter, Anna. She is also the priestess who guards the Crystal Point. She will take you there, so GO!"

The Shadow Senshi had struck the barrier full force, sending shock waves through the air and Evan to his knees. Cassandra raced to his side, as the others followed after Anna.

*   *   *

Alan could scarcely hear his heart pounding in his ears over the sound of screaming. He knew in the core of his very soul that the Earth needed him. He had not expected the pull to be so strong and now, he was feeling the full force of it.

Through the village they raced, as a tiny amount of daylight began to appear in the sky behind the clouds. They approached the towering great hall, which no doubt housed rows of communal eating tables and a large roasting pit for cooking and gathering around, as any good mead hall should have. But there was no time for curiosity and cultural exchanges. Time was of the essence and so the hall was passed by with barely a second glance. Behind the great building, the land opened up and there before them at last, was an empty space with nine enormous stones standing upright vertically in the ground, forming a large circle.

Anna stopped just before she entered it. Hardly out of breath, she turned to look at Dawn and the others. Her eyes were full of knowledge and expectancy, as though she knew what they had come to do.

"Alan," Dawn whispered, turning to face him, but he was not listening. His eyes were focused on something within the circle and he stepped forward softy.

Alan could see a large steaming black cauldron within the center of the circle. It smoked furiously, though there was no fire below it. Standing behind the cauldron, gently stirring it with a wooden paddle, was an ancient women, wrinkled beyond recognition and hunched over with the weight of her own clothing—which was nothing more than a deep purple-black robe and a green gem dangling from a rope belt. She stared through the steam at Alan and nodded. The screaming in his ears then stopped, as he stepped forward, deeper into the circle.

"What is he moving towards?" asked Robert. "His eyes are focused as though he is looking at something, or perhaps, someone . . ."

"He is with the Earth element," Dawn whispered softly, "the Crone."

*   *   *

"No!" Evan cried out as his barrier finally dissolved into a shower of shimmering lights. Cassandra was standing behind him to cast one of her own, just as the Bainbridge warriors released a flurry of arrows towards the Shadow Senshi who knocked them aside like insects.

"He's not among them!" Kage cried out.

"The one with batwings?" Itami asked, only to continue on, "Neither is Dawn, your personal target."

"Kedamono, keep them busy down there," Kage ordered. "Itami and I are going after our real goal. They are nearby and cannot hide. No, I doubt they would even if they could. Just as we have a mission, so do they!" With that, he somersaulted through the air with Itami and flew away in the direction of the great hall.

Evan caught this exchange with the corner of his eye. As he got to his feet with a groan he breathed, "Cassandra, they are heading for Dawn!"

"I will not leave you here alone with Kedamono," she said firmly. Though she was visibly shaken, her voice was steady and calm. "Dawn is strong . . . She and the others will defend themselves for a time." In her mind, Cassandra saw someone meeting their destiny. "Things are as they need to be right now," she nodded towards Evan who pursed his lips tightly.

At that moment, Kedamono slammed the ground with an earth-shattering 'thud'. His large brutish face showed no emotion aside from ignorant malice. Bringing his hands over his head, he formed two fists. In a second he brought them down to the ground, splitting the earth wide open and sending Evan, Cassandra and the Bainbridge people hurtling back with the shock wave. Water and sludge began to seep up through the crack and the land began to slowly sink inwards, as though it were being swallowed by the very earth itself.

*   *   *

"Will you look into the cauldron?" asked the Earth. Her voice was deep and raspy with age.

"Is there time for such a thing?" asked Alan, even though he felt as though time itself had stopped.

The Crone who was the Earth, chuckled. "Time enough." She indicated towards the wooden paddle. "Give it a stir."

Alan took the heavy paddle into his hands and moved it around in the sparkling liquid below. As he stared into the swirling waters he saw two rivers meandering through the land. "Where do they lead?" he asked.

"They both have the same destination, but their path differs," the Earth replied. "We both know that the time of Fadreama is ending. But for you, Alan, there are two paths you may take there. One path is you as a mortal man with all the limitations and strengths this brings. The other path has Dawn ending your life."

Alan tensed. "No! That prediction must never come to pass! I will do anything to prevent her from such an act, not for myself, but for herself. It would destroy her, I am sure."

The Earth nodded. "Then absorb me and the reason for her attack will disappear. Leave me and all will be lost."

"There really isn't a choice then," Alan said quietly.

"There is always a choice," the Earth replied. "And there is always a right and wrong choice. We tend to believe that the right choices will feel good—that is how we perceive them to be right. But sometimes, the right choices will feel bad and even painful. Yet they are right just the same. The right choice makes demands of us, whereas poor choices seldom do."

"Dawn gave up her power for my life," Alan said softly as a tear appeared in the corner of his eye. "She continues on towards the end, in spite of her own mortality."

"There is a power deeper than any you can be granted externally or by chance. It is the spark of life given to you by the Lady herself. She gave you this light and it is up to you to use it, rather than rely on external forces."

Understanding came over Alan and he swallowed hard. "We are one then," he whispered. "The Earth and I, we are one and there is no room for demon blood."

Using his hand, Alan scooped up some of the liquid within the cauldron and drank. Immediately he felt a great warmth surge though his body. It was cleansing and overpowering. He felt something break—some cord, some tie, some chain—it was the blood of the Vampires. It was gone. He was Alan. Alan and the Element Earth. But the Earth would not save him. No, rather, he would save the Earth.

"What is that light?" Mizu wondered, as the group stared at Alan, alone in the center of the circle.

"He has absorbed the Earth," Ian observed, feeling the Air's happiness.

Dawn held a hand to her heart. "Something else has happened . . ."

Robert touched her shoulder. "You really love Alan, don't you?" he asked.

Dawn nodded her head slowly. "I am sorry, Robert. You have always protected me and been so good a friend. But my heart, it has always belonged to my Shepherd Boy. Maybe it has been confused, but it has always been with him."

Robert nodded slowly. "In another place, in another time, then. The Power is not so cruel . . . Surely you will be shared and others can enjoy happiness if they have patience and wait their turn."

Dawn gave him a small smile. "Perhaps."

Anna shouted something in Bainbridge and pointed as Alan began to walk towards them. He reached out his arms to Dawn and she rushed forward to meet him. Staring into his eyes, Dawn saw something that had been hidden for a long time—a human soul.

"Alan," she whispered, "you are human."

"The Earth could not reside in a body with Vampire blood," Alan explained. "I knew what I had to do—Dawn you inspired me—I let her purge me of the demonic. Do not fear the predictions. It shall not come to pass." He stared intently at Dawn.

The others looked on in confusion, but Dawn threw herself into his arms without a word.

Suddenly Anna screamed. Before anyone realized what had just taken place, Robert—who was suddenly standing before Dawn and Alan—crumpled to the ground. A ribbon of blood showed the clean slash of a scythe across his chest.

There, seemingly out of thin air, stood Kage and Itami.

CHAPTER 26

Kage's Choice

"**N**O!" DAWN SCREAMED, FALLING to her knees and cradling Robert's head. "He saved us," Alan murmured as a wave of nausea overtook him.

"Dead . . ." Dawn whispered as she felt her body go numb. "Oh Robert . . ." A gush of tears found their way down her cheeks and splashed upon that of the dead lord.

Kage let out a mighty laugh. "I have you now and if I have to pick off every one of your friends first, I will." He glowered at Dawn. *This girl has made a fool of me for the last time! Ralston will see! He will have to grant me freedom!*

Dawn felt a knot tighten in her stomach and her head spun. *I have no power, Alan has no power, Ian has no power...Only Mizu has her magic.* To her surprise, Alan pulled out his crossbow.

"It is rather ordinary now, but I am willing to try."

Mizu glowed with her Glintel power. "I will sink him myself if I have to," she said with determination.

Dawn's eyes glistened. *Everyone . . . I will not lose you!* Laying Robert's head gently upon the ground and placing a small kiss on his forehead, Dawn got to her feet.

"No one can save you this time!" Kage screamed with rage.

Dawn could see the dark aura around him and to her it suddenly seemed so filled with sadness that it nearly broke her heart. *He is so sad . . . So very, very, sad . . .* "Stop!" she said to the others. "Do not fire upon them!"

"Dawn, are you crazy?" Mizu asked almost angrily.

Alan immediately lowered his bow and said, "Trust her!"

Dawn gave Alan a quick look and then raced towards the Shadow Senshi who had backed off a few paces. Kage was suddenly confused by her apparent insanity. *What is that girl doing?*

"I can free you!" she cried and her words echoed through the air and into Kage and Itami's souls. "You are slaves and prisoners! But I can set you free! You do not have to die as slaves!"

Kage narrowed his eyes. *This girl is insane . . .*

It was at this point that Dawn began to glow.

* * *

"I will cut Kedamono from this world!" Evan grunted as Cassandra helped him to his feet. They were bruised and bloodied from a battle that was more like a massacre. "I will slice through the Synergy which binds him!"

Cassandra paused, "Wait a moment. Something has happened. No, something *is* happening! Do not do anything yet. See, over the great hall! That light! It is a bright light . . . Dawn!"

Kedamono looked towards the light from his path of destruction and death. Something stirred in his cold heart and he fled towards the Crystal Point. Meanwhile, the land had begun to sink inward where Kedamono had split the earth in two. It glubbed and bubbled as Bainbridge began to disappear, taking the bodies of the Pegasus-Unicorns and Bainbridge soliders—including that of Bran—with it.

Evan could only look at Cassandra and say, "We must hurry."

* * *

"The end is coming," Dawn said calmly. Her entire body was glowing with a light that emanated from within. "But you do not have to experience your last hours as a slave. I can free you. I can break Ralston's hold on your soul."

"What is she talking about?" Mizu asked Ian. She grasped his hand tightly and tried not to look at Robert.

"It is her power," Ian whispered in awe. "This is Dawn. This is what she can do when the moment is right."

Kage and Itami stood seemingly paralyzed, but the suspicion never left their angry features. "I have had enough of everything!" Kage screamed. "I want you gone!"

"You want me gone, or Ralston wants me gone? Whose will do you serve?" Dawn asked gently. She moved towards them until she stood a mere step away.

At that moment, Kedamono arrived and stared with wonder in his large eyes. With his lumbering gait, he came to stand beside his companions—an uncharacteristic look of intrigue on his face.

Soon after, Evan and Cassandra appeared, breathing hard. Evan blanched when he saw Robert.

"Kedamono," Dawn offered turning to him, "I will free you. Do you want to be free? I do not ask for anything in return."

Kage and Itami watched the great brute with a mixture of suspicion and anticipation.

"You have been sorely misused and abused," Dawn said sympathetically. "In this world there is so much pain, but it will end shortly. Why not experience freedom, for once in your life? Let go of Ralston. He does not hold you anymore. It is *you* who cling to *him*. Let him go." She stepped closer.

"Dawn . . ." Evan breathed as he tried to turn his attention away from his fallen companion. Then, to the others he said, "Bainbridge is sinking. We have to go very soon."

"She will do this," Alan said tensely. "She will free them."

"Then what?" Mizu asked. "How do we get out of here? Where do we go?"

"Have faith," came Alan's reply.

It was Kedamono who came closer. Dawn smiled. "Kedamono. You are free. Go where you will. Enjoy what is left of Fadreama." She reached out and touched his massive arm. A light surrounded him and the tension in his great muscles relaxed. With amazing lightness, he floated in the air and just like that, he left. That was it. He left.

Itami looked on in amazement. "Let Ralston do what he will. I want to be free."

Again, Dawn smiled and touched Itami's head. "Go in peace. Find peace with yourself and with who you are. Even demons deserve to be free. Ralston cannot touch you now." And Itami was surrounded and penetrated by the white light. With a lopsided smile, he too flew off in the opposite direction of Kedamono.

Now Dawn was faced with Kage, who seemed to be fighting an internal battle of sorts. "Kage," she said softly. "Is it you who hate me so?"

"I hate everyone," he whispered, shaking. "I hate the world for being so cruel . . ."

"Let it go," Dawn soothed. Her light brightened. "Do something just for yourself for once. Go where you wish. Do not think about anything else, just you. Have you ever done anything for yourself?"

A light came over his face. "N . . . No." Kage seemed to have a revelation. "Always . . . serving, obeying . . . Fear . . . Afraid. So afraid."

Dawn nodded with understanding. "The world can be scary on your own, I know. Sometimes we think giving up our freedom in exchange for security or power is best. But then we miss out on so much . . . We miss out on living our own lives. Perhaps we don't always know what is out there, but at least we can explore it at will.

There is so very much in this world. That is why my mother loved it. That is why I love it too."

"I want to know it . . . is there time?"

"There is time enough," Dawn whispered and touched his hand.

"Thank you for seeing what no one else could." Kage was the only one of the three to say these words.

As Kage flew off into the sky, Dawn felt the world spinning around her. Immediately Alan was at her side supporting her. She looked up into his face and whispered, "It is time to go back . . . to where it all began." There was a flash of light and everyone disappeared, just as Bainbridge—and Robert—sank into nothingness.

CHAPTER 27

Back To Where It All Began

THE FORGOTTEN FOREST WAS both a place of refuge and of danger. While it could protect and shelter, it could also endanger and expose. This was a place that demanded respect. It was also a place of paradox—both a beginning and an ending point. It was amongst these sacred trees that the Goddess Incarnate, Alice, had been nurtured and raised for the first 15 years of her life. It was also sacred ground for the elements—specifically that of Spirit, which was likely why Dawn had somehow transported not only herself and her friends, but also Anna, the sole survivor of the Bainbridge people.

Dawn stood tall and unwavering, despite having exerted such power. The others merely stared at her in awe. Who was this child of a goddess? What would she do in these final hours, when Ralston was sure to show up?

"Oh Robert," Dawn whispered, her eyes glassy. They stood within a circular clearing of trees.

The others made no reply. What could they say? Robert was gone and soon enough, they would be too. There was no use in crying.

Dawn then shook her head and said, "Do you know what grounds these are?" She did not wait for an answer. "My mother lived here. There was . . . a large manor, right there," she indicated towards the center of the clearing. "Nissim's magic wove a childhood here for her and her sisters." Dawn knelt down and touched the soil with reverence. "The time for Revolution has arrived and it will happen here, in the Forgotten Forest of Algernon." She then looked up at her friends who were solemnly staring at her. "This is where we make our stand and end it once and for all."

"We—and the Elements—are with you, Dawn," Evan offered bravely. "You have our support, Cousin." Though he spoke strongly, there was a sadness within his eyes that could not be entirely hidden. Two lifetimes of finding true love, only to have it ripped away both times . . . It was almost too much to endure.

"He is right, Dawn," Mizu nodded, knowing full well that she would live forever, no matter what happened in Fadreama. *I am going to mourn for all eternity . . .*

"Everyone," Dawn said as she felt a great power awaken and pulse through her veins, "Spirit is here. This is a Crystal Point."

Alan touched Dawn gently on the shoulder. "Do you feel the Element here somewhere? Do you see her?"

Dawn smiled slowly and looked up at the sky which was turning dark again. In her heart, she suddenly knew. "I see her alright. I *am* Spirit." Her eyes sparkled. "I have always *been* Spirit. Spirit's stronghold is here, but *she* wasn't. *She* is *me.* She is alive. I have held her since the day I was born. Somehow . . . She incarnated as a human, perhaps foreseeing the end."

"Certainly it explains a great deal," Cassandra nodded. "And why not? Spirit incarnate as a goddess incarnate's child!" she laughed. "The universe is a strange place, is it not?"

"Madame Iris must have known all along," Ian mused thoughtfully.

Cassandra tensed at the mention of her mentor's name. Sensing this, Evan spoke up, "So, Dawn . . . What now?"

"Cassandra and Anna," Dawn began, but was interrupted by a great noise from the trees. There, pushing her way through the underbrush, was the Priestess Lily, along with Boudicca and the other priestesses.

"Dawn!" Lily exclaimed, hailing her niece. She and the others made their way quickly through the clearing. "Thank goodness we made it before Ralston!"

Dawn quickly embraced both her aunts—Lily and Andrea. "You all came!" she exclaimed and then lowered her voice. "Please, give me the strength to do what I must."

"Oh, Dawn," Lily whispered looking into the girl's eyes. "You have more of Alice's determination than you realize." Then, shaking her head she said, "Those that went before us, they are still with us and will support us all now. We are never destroyed, Dawn. Do you understand?"

She nodded and there was a light within her eyes. "Yes, I do."

"Everyone!" Lily commanded. "Surround the clearing! We must maintain this ground for as long as possible!" Now Lily's eyes sparked. *I have survived only for this day!* "For the Goddess!" The priestesses quickly spaced themselves around the clearing.

"This is our darkest hour," Boudicca said, hesitating before she took her place. "I am honoured to share that hour with you all."

"And I you," Dawn replied with a small smile. "Good luck to you."

"Be not afraid," Boudicca nodded and joined her women.

"Cassandra," Lily spoke up. "Please join our circle. It will take all the energy we can muster to maintain it." Her gaze wandered over to Anna. "And her as well. I can see that she serves the Goddess too."

Even without knowing the language, Anna seemed to understand. With a quick nod to everyone, she sprinted off towards Boudicca. Perhaps Anna knew better than anyone else that this day had been coming.

Now Evan stood before Cassandra and held both of her hands tightly. They were staring into each other's eyes, but not speaking. This was enough. The bond between them was one of honest and true love. Yet in their hearts, they knew it could never be. Their time, like Darius and Kiara before them, had come and gone.

"I will find you," Evan said firmly. "And if you still want me—"

Cassandra cut him off by putting a finger to his lips. "I wish I could say do not make such promises . . . but I do not want to say it. All I will say is, I will be waiting."

"Evan," Dawn said softly, "it is time. Take up your place in the south, Guardian of the sacred fire. Keeper of passion, will and power."

Evan gave Cassandra one last look, before turning and walking several steps away from Dawn, facing the south. Lily took Cassandra by the hand and led her to the outer rim of the clearing with the other priestesses.

Dawn now turned to Mizu. "My friend, please take your place in the west, as the only true Guardian of Water. You, who guard emotion, magic and love."

Mizu hesitated before Ian. "Ian . . ."

"I love you," Ian said and kissed her. "Now, go." His eyes had glazed over.

Without another word, Mizu walked several steps to the west of Dawn, who stood in the center of the clearing.

"Alan," Dawn's voice faltered slightly as she gazed into his solemn, human eyes. "I will love you for all eternity," she said softly.

"Until we meet again," Alan said before launching himself into a kiss with her.

When they parted, Dawn said quickly, "Alan, Guardian of the Earth, please stand true in the north. You who represents life, stability, support and strength."

As Alan moved to the north, Dawn took a deep breath and turned to Ian. "I need you to complete the circle, Cousin."

"You can count on it," he replied with resolution.

"Ian! The East! Guardian of the Air! You who gives us creativity, music and voice!"

Ian took his place, while trying not to look back at Mizu, who stood resolutely opposite him.

Dawn now stood alone in the center of the clearing with two circles around her—the smaller circle of elements and the larger circle of priestesses. The dusk had turned into night and the forest was cast into darkness. A cold wind swept in from nowhere and Dawn began to glow.

Ralston's Dark Mind

"**T**HAT LITTLE WENCH!" RALSTON seethed through Lance's perfectly straight, pearly teeth. "What is she planning to do now? What can she possibly do at this point? Certainly she has gained the power of the elements through her friends and is herself the so-called 'Spirit' element, but really, what can she hope to actually *achieve*?"

"Her mind is quite unknowable and complex," the Creature spoke up thoughtfully.

They stood just outside the clearing in the Forgotten Forest and were unobserved by the others. Ralston was gripping the side of a tree and the Creature was leaning his shoulder upon another.

"Without knowing her objective, it is difficult to plot a course of action . . ." Ralston rubbed his chin absently. "So many times I have tried to just kill her. Why is that so difficult?" He slammed his fist into his hand.

"She is fairly resistant to mind-control," the Creature continued along his own line of thought. "Perhaps you need to invite her into your mind. Let her see what lies there . . ." He narrowed his eyes. "That should crush her hope and spirit. Invite her in, unless of course, you are afraid of what she might find." The Creature gave Ralston an odd look of challenge.

"See that you don't cross the line," Ralston snapped. "In what world would I fear Dawn? Certainly not this one! She shall come inside, but she shall never return!" He laughed manically and turned violently to the Creature. "And now that I've no more use for you . . ." Like a monster, Ralston lunged at the Creature, absorbing him in an instant—thus taking in Magica as well. Oddly enough, the Creature had been smiling, even as Ralston absorbed him. It was this smile that Ralston could not erase from his mind, for the smile had been that of Magica.

"Ralston," came a voice from the darkness.

"Get lost, Chartreuse," he growled back. "I am busy. Don't you have a mead hall to entertain?"

Chartreuse laughed but it was a sad sort of laugh. "Once, Ralston Radburn, I loved you."

"That was a very long time ago," he said more quietly. "That time is gone. I am not what you loved. I am different now."

"Always your ambition," Chartreuse said sadly. "Your ambition was more important than anything or anyone!"

"You do not love me," Ralston said tiredly. "You loved someone else . . . Goodbye!"

With that said, Ralston disappeared, only to reappear within Dawn's circle of light, leaving Chartreuse on the outside looking in. "Oh Ralston," she whispered softly.

* * *

"Ralston Radburn," Dawn breathed, as Ralston stood directly before her.

"Are you afraid, little Dawn? There is no one now to stand between us," Ralston mocked.

For a brief moment, Dawn could see the withered old man that Ralston truly was, beneath the handsome disguise of her mother's cousin, Lord Lance de Felda. Her face formed a pitying expression. *He is so frail!* "Oh, Ralston, you really are just a sad lonely being."

Taken aback, Ralston snarled, "You are about to be absorbed into my darkness, princess. There is no use in fighting it, so just give in to it. If you do so, there will be little pain. You have caused me far too much trouble in the past. We end this here and now. You and all your power shall become a part of me."

Dawn laughed lightly, further frustrating and confusing Ralston. "Do not fool yourself into thinking you can contain my light," Dawn replied calmly. Despite her situation, she felt neither panic nor fear. *I feel the power of my friends surrounding me . . . And I feel my mother protecting me. Everyone, even those that have moved on from this plane are with me. Give me your strength everyone!* "You may try, oh Sad One," Dawn smiled. "You are welcome to try and absorb me. We shall see what comes of it." With that, she reached out and took Ralston's hand. "Try."

Giving his head a shake from the shock and ease of it all, Ralston ruthlessly yanked Dawn towards him, causing her to instantly vanish into his body.

"Dawn . . ." Alan whispered, feeling a bead of sweat drip from his brow as he tried to hold the sacred circle together and maintain a holy space. "Fadreama is coming apart . . ."

* * *

Dawn stood alone in a very dark, cold place. There was nothing around her at all. It was a complete void. She did not even know if she stood upon ground, or hovered in the air.

"This place," she whispered, "it is empty, yet filled with such sadness." Her aura glowed brighter and her lacy fairy wings shimmered out. Though Dawn had not noticed, her clothing had transformed into a gauzy gown of shimmering prismatic light.

"The mind of Ralston . . ." she whispered. "The sadness . . . He is so very lonely." A tear escaped from her eye and fell like a glittering diamond into the abyss.

"Do not cry, sweet Dawn," came a tiny voice.

"Glims! My dearest Glims!" Dawn whispered, as a tiny light appeared before her. Sure enough in the void hovered Glimmer, the pixie, and behind her were the many people Ralston had absorbed, including Dusk and even Magica herself.

"We have been waiting for you," Glimmer said with a tinkle. "We knew you would come for us. *I knew*." The pixie flew up to Dawn and touched her tear streaked face. "I told everyone not to lose hope. We will be able to find our peace soon."

Dawn nodded. "Yes, I have come into this void to help you move on and find peace. Ralston absorbed you because he is so very, very, lonely. He is a sad being, perhaps the saddest being that has ever existed. To cope with such feelings, he tried to fill his void with power, darkness and ultimately, people. Yet this void of sadness cannot be filled by any of these means. I think . . . I think he knows this. He is still not satisfied."

"There is someone here you must talk to, Dawn," Glimmer indicated behind her.

There stood Magica, but there was something different about her now. The malice was gone from her eyes. She was a woman who had been broken and given time to look inward as to why. She came forward and gave a smile of relief. "Dawn, you have finally come. I had to push Ralston, but he took the bait. I knew it would be okay if you came . . . that we might have a chance. When I arrived, Glimmer told us again . . . she said you would come. She said you would save even those who have no right to be saved."

"Magica . . ." Dawn began. She searched her heart for feelings of anger or vengeance against this woman who had destroyed her family and home. Yet there was oddly nothing of the sort within her. "You were a pawn of Ralston's, Magica. Ill used long before I came into this world. You did what you did because you too were lost and alone."

Magica took Dawn's hands and knelt before her, as tears flowed from her eyes. "My life was based on deception and hate, but now I see . . . Vengeance blinds us to the truth and it poisons our minds. It latches on to that little bit of darkness that exists in everyone's hearts and it fuels it. Your mother was much stronger than I and I am sorry for what—"

Dawn interrupted her. "Do not speak of it, Magica. It is over and done. I did not come here to heap blame upon anyone. I came here to illuminate the void and fill that part of Ralston he could not fill with power."

Magica's son, Dusk, came to stand beside his mother. She touched his shoulder gently, in a way that a mother should. Dusk smiled at Dawn. "Though I deceived you greatly, I honestly did admire you, with good reason. There is something pure about you that cannot be comprehended easily. I think Alan is lucky to have your heart."

"Dusk . . ." she began, "I wish things could have been different for you. We all deserved better, but . . . this is how it is. We cannot change what has happened, but we can control what we do right now."

There was a rumbling amongst the crowd of absorbed people behind Magica and Dusk. "So, Dawn, what are we going to do?" asked Glimmer.

"We are going to act collectively against Ralston. Every one of you is going to assert your will for peace." Dawn felt her heart skip a beat, for she did not know where this plan had come from, but she felt that it was right. "You are going to *will* yourself free and towards peace. Though you can never again live in the world of Fadreama, you can at least move on to some other plane. Together you can all deny Ralston." A flush of colour came to her cheeks as she tried to rouse the crowd. Up into the darkness she exclaimed, "Deny Ralston's will! Ralston! We deny you and this void! These people are not simply stuffing for your emptiness! They are not for you Ralston! Not now or ever! They are not what you want! Let them go or they will force you to!"

The crowd began to chant and one voice excelled louder than the rest. It was Lord Lance de Felda. He gave Dawn a winning smile. "This is my body and I will take it back now! RALSTON!" he screamed. "I am not your puppet! I am FREE!"

*   *   *

Ralston still stood within the circle Dawn had formed with her friends. In truth, he found he could not leave it. The power of the

Elements had trapped him within its walls. A barrier of synergy was surging between Alan, Evan, Ian and Mizu that could not be broken, even by his magic.

Suddenly Ralston clutched at his head and dropped to his knees. He looked at his hands in horror. *They are fading . . . This body is being reclaimed and is turning to dust. But I will never go without a fight! If I must fade at last, this wretched world shall crumble with me!* Summoning his dark energy, Ralston set off shock waves throughout Fadreama. All over the land, in all countries, the ground began to shake and the world, literally, began to crumble.

"What's going on?" asked Andrea, as she was knocked off her feet.

"Ralston is destroying Fadreama," Lily whispered with tears in her eyes.

"Chartreuse!" Cassandra cried.

Chartreuse emerged from the surrounding trees like a cool breeze. Her face was greatly pained. "I'm afraid there is nothing we can do but wait and see what Dawn does. Only she has the power to face Ralston. I am sure she has the power . . . Ralston . . ."

Cassandra looked intense. "You once saw something good in him, didn't you?"

Chartreuse laughed. "If you can call what I saw 'good'. Yes, I was once close to Ralston, but he is so very empty and not even what I had to offer could fill that gap. Fulfillment comes from within, not without."

It was then that poor Anna, last of the Bainbridge tribes spoke up. She declared something in her language, to which Cassandra nodded and translated, "She says that everything comes from within. Everything on the outside is just illusion. All that is true is inside."

"Look," Chartreuse whispered, as Lance began to turn to dust and blow away.

"Dawn . . ." Lily whispered.

CHAPTER 29

Filling the Void

"**D**AWN, OUR TIME IS short now," Glimmer smiled at her companion, so very, very, proud. "Your mother, she is so pleased with you. I can feel her energy calling us to the next plane."

Dawn smiled and tried not to cry. "You are free now, Glims." She wiped away a tear with the back of her hand and sniffed. "But I cannot join you right away. I have things to do first."

"I will be waiting for you when you are ready," Glimmer smiled. "I knew you would come for us. I told everyone so. The greatest joy of my life was being your guardian. For that, I thank you." Glimmer then faded away. The others were fading as well. There was a great sense of peace among them all as Ralston was no longer able to hold onto them.

"Do what you must," Magica nodded. "We are all indebted to you for more than you can ever know." Her eyes were shining. "In all my sad life, I have never known such peace." She faded away, as did all the other absorbed souls. Within minutes, Dawn was left alone in the dark void. There was absolutely nothing around her and the silence was deafening.

"It's so dark and cold," Dawn whispered to herself and hugged her arms. "But there is something . . . no . . . *someone* I must find." She peered into the darkness. "Ralston . . ."

It was then that she saw a small figure. It was that of a little boy with a thick shock of brown hair. He was standing all alone and he was crying. His small body shook with his racking, yet silent sobs. Dawn came to him from behind and placed a hand on his shaking shoulder. "Ralston, it is okay."

The child turned to look up at Dawn. "How can you say that?" he demanded in a childish voice. "How can you say it is okay? I am so lonely! I have nothing! I have no one! I am lost in this darkness and there is no way out."

Dawn began to glow white, as her heart went out to this boy who had been called a demon. "They say you sold your soul to the

Fallen One. But perhaps we shouldn't be so quick to believe what others say. It is a fault of humanity I suppose. We believe words, often with no proof at all. This can be used for good or bad." Her light grew brighter.

"Yes . . ." Ralston began. "They said things . . . over and over. I believed them. I wanted to feel something. I took and took and took. But the more I took, the more I wanted. Nothing filled the void. It was always a hole. Always empty and I was always wanting."

Sparks began to flicker around Dawn as she seemed to be glittering. "The Lady gives every being a special gift. It is the gift of light and love that she bestows upon us all. It is within us and can never be lost. But, sometimes, we can forget. We forget about that divine light within and it recedes into hiding, yet is never gone. It is that light you were searching for, Ralston. That light within that says you are a good and worthy being is what will fill this void. Ralston . . . look!"

Within her hands, Dawn held a glowing sphere of light. "Ralston . . . if you touch this light . . . if you give up that greed that has brought you to this point, you can be healed. You don't have to live in this void. I am offering you fulfillment without asking for anything in return."

The child suddenly looked ashamed and angry. "But everything I have done and continue to do . . . Fadreama is crumbling and it cannot be stopped. I have done so much evil, Dawn. How can you possibly forgive and heal me of that? When I have done *so much wrong?* I caused so much pain. I delighted in the suffering of others, including yourself. *How can you forgive that?*"

Though his words were true, Dawn felt herself smiling. "No one ever told you that you are a worthy being . . . just as worthy as anyone else. You were worthy of love but never received it when you most needed it. And so you came to shun it, even when Chartreuse would have given it to you. You were so scarred; you could not see love when it was in front of you. I do not blame you, Ralston. Let me heal your soul. Can you accept healing?"

"You don't care about what I have done?"

"I care, Ralston, but I choose to see past it. I choose to see that light the Lady gave you. I choose to see what Chartreuse sees. That is why I am here. I see what most others cannot. I see it within my hands Ralston. This light is yours. Touch it and you will remember."

Uncertainly, Ralston reached out his hand and placed it upon the sphere of light which pulsed and suddenly expanded to light up the void. There was whiteness and sparkling illumination everywhere. The darkness was gone, replaced by a clean fresh world of sun.

Ralston blinked and looked around in surprise. "This . . . is me?"

Dawn nodded, her eyes shining. "This is your right, given to you by the Lady. Do you remember?"

"I feel so . . . full . . . it is more than I can describe," the child whispered. "I want for nothing. This is everything. It is unlike anything I have ever known."

"It is your true self," Dawn beamed happily. "This light . . . it is us. It is everyone. It fills us with strength and happiness. It guides us to what is true and leads us away from material illusion. Take away everything and this bliss is what we are left with. It is pure spirit and higher self. It is the essence of our being."

Ralston gave her a strange look. "But what is it?"

"Love," she smiled. "Pure and simple love. Love is all that is left now." She looked up. "But I must return before I can enter into my own light. The Twilight Revolution has began, Ralston. Be in peace."

CHAPTER 30

The End of Fadreama

"**D**awn!" Alan exclaimed when he saw her suddenly reappear in the clearing and fall to the ground.

All around them, Fadreama was breaking into pieces and blowing away into the wind. Thus far the sacred circles had kept everyone safe, but they would not be able to hold on for long.

"Alan!" Lily called from the outer circle. "We will hold it for as long as possible! Go to her"!

Without a second thought, Alan broke the inner circle and in moments held the limp princess in his arms. Evan, Ian and Mizu crowded around in concern. "Dawn! Dawn please wake up!"

Dawn would not open her eyes just yet. She knew that she must, but she needed just a few moments more. Her mother now stood before her . . . not Syoho . . . Alice. They were in that ethereal plane between consciousness and unconsciousness. It was the only place left where they could meet.

Alice smiled broadly and it was clear how immensely proud she was of her only daughter. "Dawn."

Dawn flew into her arms and they embraced. "I wasn't sure he would listen," Dawn admitted.

"You did what you came here to do," Alice said softly. "You came here to save us all. In the end, it was not The Lady or any of the Nine, or even Syoho. It was you, Dawn. You saved us with your unconditional love. It is more than any of us could have done."

Dawn gazed up at her mother's lovely face. "I was fortunate to know love in so many forms. Not everyone is so lucky." She paused and continued, "And now, what of Fadreama? I can feel it breaking into pieces all around! And the people are disappearing with it . . ."

Alice looked a little sad. "Fadreama is going the way of many other worlds before it. When a world becomes overwhelmed and overshadowed by its problems, it fades away to await rebirth. Nothing is ever destroyed, only transformed. And you, Dawn, have the power. The second stone I gave you . . . it is not an Elf Stone. You guessed this already. It is an *intention* Dawn—an intention to do with what you will." Now Alice smiled. "But I think you already know what you will do."

Dawn nodded. "Yes, I have an intention."

"Use it well, my daughter. We shall meet again."

"We shall all meet again."

Dawn's blue eyes opened and she found herself staring up at Alan. "You're alive!" he cried, hugging her.

"Of course," she mumbled, straining to find her voice—she had been on so many different planes, it took a moment to feel this plane's frequency. "I must get up . . . Fadreama is dying."

Alan and Evan helped Dawn to her feet. The Forgotten Forest seemed peaceful, except for a faint rumbling in the ground.

"Ralston is gone," Evan spoke up. "We saw Lance's body disintegrate and Ralston's spirit walk into the light. I don't know how you managed it, Dawn, but you are truly amazing."

"I only wish . . . no," Dawn shook her head. "I have only one wish, one intention. I will not waste it on selfish thoughts."

"What do we do now?" Mizu asked. "What will happen when the earthquakes make it here? The priestesses cannot hold this space forever."

"We will fade out of this world," Evan spoke up softly.

"I cannot fade away," Ian said stubbornly. "I have to live. The Sisters told me that I must live at any cost to tell the truth."

A cold wind swept by and blew through Dawn's sparkling hair. A voice seemed to whisper in her ear and she closed her eyes with a nod. "The Goddess Nalopa has something to offer." Dawn could fairly hear the ocean waves in her mind. Scarcely knowing what she was doing, Dawn raised her hand and a portal opened. Within the portal was the sea. "It is the immortal sea," she said softly. "This is the land of Mizu's birth." Dawn turned to Mizu, "It is time for you to return home."

"But . . . Ian," Mizu stumbled. "I . . ." She had known this moment would come and she could sense Nalopa calling. "I can never be like the other Glintels now," she whispered.

"You need not go alone," Dawn said. "Nalopa's reward for your bravery is to bring Ian with you . . . into immortality."

"Ian!" Mizu ran into his arms.

Looking over his shoulder, Ian said, "Everyone will know what happened here. It will not be forgotten. My purpose is truth." His handsome face looked very solemn and there were tears in his eyes. *Everyone I know will be gone . . . But this is my destiny . . .* "For eternity

I will give truth to those who seek it and even those who do not. I never forget."

"So be it, Cousin," Dawn whispered. "But you must go now. There is so little time." She hugged Ian and Mizu tightly. "Friends do not bid each other goodbye. This is no exception."

Tears fell from Mizu's eyes and she blinked them quickly away. I wish every Glintel could know what I know . . ."

"Paint a nice image of me," Evan told Ian with a forced smile. "Make me a great warrior."

"That is the truth," Ian said with a nod.

"Don't romance too many Glintels now!" Alan teased with a forced smile.

Ian shook his head. "Don't think that will be an issue now."

"You have to go." Dawn ushered Ian and Mizu to the portal. "Go and please, be happy with your choice."

With that, the two passed into the immortal realm and the thunderous earthquakes grew louder. The trees around them began to snap and break as the world of Fadreama drew to a close. The priestesses began to tremble as their powers started to weaken.

"We are starting to fade," Chartreuse spoke up, examining her hand. It was semi-translucent.

"It is approaching faster than I had thought," Cassandra mused softly and looked back at Evan.

"Be brave, ladies, and hold on for as long as you can!" Lily said sternly. *Sisters, I will be with you soon!*

"What's that in your hand?" asked Alan, noticing Dawn's clutched right hand.

"The stone my mother gave me," she whispered. "It holds a very special intention. It is the last thing I can do for Fadreama and for everyone who wants a part of it."

"What is it?" Alan pressed as he held Dawn's free hand.

"We are born of the same land," she whispered. "We will meet again and again . . . all of us, I promise. There will always be both dark and light. We cannot have one without the other. I cannot eliminate half of our souls. But I can let us try again and again to get it right. I can let the earth try again. We are all born of it and we will all learn together." No tears fell from her dry eyes, for Dawn's entire being was focused upon her intention—she would not let it go. *It must come to pass!*

The small group stood close together in the center of the Forgotten Forest, lending each other courage for what was to come.

Dawn, Evan, Alan and the priestesses were the last souls left in Fadreama.

"Evan," Cassandra called from the edge of the circle.

"Again and again," Evan called back as he watched her fade away. Evan held his breath and knew that what Dawn had said was true. *We are born of the same land and we will meet . . . again and again . . .*

"We are fading." Alan's voice was difficult to hear. With the priestess circle gone, Fadreama was disappearing fast. The trees of the Forgotten Forest were gone . . . All that remained was a tiny patch of ground where Dawn and the others stood.

"This . . . is . . . . is . . . ." Dawn tried to speak. Voices could no longer carry in the airless world. The earth moved and heaved, as the Forgotten Forest crumbled into oblivion. The young people in the clearing faded out, and the last thing Dawn did was to look into Alan's eyes as she held the crystal clear stone aloft and released her intention . . . .

One word echoed through the nothingness . . . . One word whispered through the cosmos and void. One intention filled with power cried out and manifested its intent: REBIRTH. An explosion burst out of nowhere within the void, initiated by nothing more than a thought. From this, came life.

CHAPTER 31

Born of the Same World

A SMART LOOKING YOUNG LADY with shiny brown hair pinned up into a loose bun was standing calmly at a train station in western Japan. It was a quiet residential station used only by the people who lived in the immediate area. The hour was quite early and the sun was just barely starting to turn the sky pink. In the distance, a group of crows cawed out noisily as they flapped about in the pine trees.

The lady wore a grey business skirt and neatly pressed white blouse with feminine lace bows and a bit of ruffle. She had a black woolen autumn jacket on, as November had just begun. A fashionable shoulder bag was balanced neatly on her forearm, just as she balanced carefully on her black high heels. She glanced down at her silver wristwatch and sighed. A sudden noise caused her to turn around. She gave a slight nod and said a demure, "Ohayo gozaimasu."

The young man who had just stepped out onto the platform nodded back with an appropriate response. His polished black shoes made slight tapping sounds as he paced about. He was dressed in the attire of a salary man—business suit, tie and suitcase. He seemed a bit agitated as he leaned from foot to foot. Finally, as though gathering his courage, he spoke, "Excuse me, but I can speak English."

The lady turned around again and smiled warmly. "I had no idea. I see you here every morning and you have never spoken to me in English before, nor Japanese for that matter."

Putting a hand behind his head and blushing a little, the man gave a nervous laugh. "I guess I was just being shy. I teach English— well, sort of. I edit English documents at an office."

"Oh I teach English too," the lady offered with a bright smile. "I teach at a girls' school. The school sponsored my visa to come here. But . . . I felt the need to come all my life. I really can't explain it, but, here I am."

"Maybe it is your destiny," the man joked, feeling slightly more comfortable. "My name is Ikeda Aki," he offered, stating his family name and then first name as propriety dictated.

The lady nodded and smiled. "Pleased to meet you. My name is Lumiere, Sofia." She extended a hand and continued, "Please call me Sofia."

"If we are to forgo formalities, then you must call me Aki," he insisted, taking her hand. As he did so, a strange sensation of familiarity came over him. He could not explain it.

"I feel . . ." Sofia began, "that somehow we are on terms of familiarity already. Do you feel that too?"

Aki nodded. "Yes . . . It is the strangest feeling. We haven't met before and other than this train station, I don't think I have seen you anywhere else."

Sofia shook her head, as though trying to clear it. "I sense there is something, just on the edge of my consciousness that I would like to remember, but the harder I try, the more it recedes into the darkness."

Aki stared carefully at this lovely lady before him. She looked to be in her mid-twenties, the same as himself. Sofia was different—she was foreign—but there was something else, something he couldn't quite put his finger on.

"I suppose we are being quite silly, aren't we," Sofia laughed suddenly. "There is no need for such seriousness. Whatever there was before does not matter. All that matters is right now. We have met and we are now familiar." She blinked her blue eyes as the sunlight broke over the rooftops and illuminated the sky.

Aki came to stand directly beside Sofia. He was close enough to feel her gentle breathing and he smiled as a peaceful sense of calm came over him—like something inside his soul was completed.

"I don't think the dawn has ever looked so beautiful," Sofia whispered, unconsciously leaning closer towards Aki.

"It's a new day," he said.

"Yes," replied Sofia confidently, "it is."

Epilogue

An excerpt from *The Book of Truths* by the great Bard, Ian:

What could not be brought down by brute force, was brought down by love, understanding and compassion. Dawn did more with her heart, than those wielding all the power of the world and beyond. So few of us can love that unconditionally and it was that great intention of love, which saved us all. For everything begins with an intention. All things great and small start out as mere thoughts—we should always be mindful of this, for we create our world based on this principle. Thoughts of fear manifest fear, but thoughts of love . . .

From Dawn's intention of love and compassion, we can all live again—try again, in a new world with new circumstances. All that was true and pure and good in Fadreama, will come to pass again—Dawn saw to that. Some bonds cannot be broken and nothing is ever lost. There is transformation on the outside but the inside—the higher self—remains untouched. Our highest self cannot change, only the shell that gives us the vehicle to experience the manifest can. All of us, we are born of the same source and we will meet again and again . . . and again. The miracle of transformation.

'I will find my way back to you, always.'